Arthur Beaman Simonds

American song

A Collection of Representative American Poems with Analytical and Critical Strudies

of the Writers

Arthur Beaman Simonds

American song
A Collection of Representative American Poems with Analytical and Critical Strudies of the Writers

ISBN/EAN: 9783744708104

Printed in Europe, USA, Canada, Australia, Japan

Cover: Foto ©Andreas Hilbeck / pixelio.de

More available books at **www.hansebooks.com**

AMERICAN SONG

A COLLECTION OF REPRESENTATIVE AMERICAN
POEMS, WITH ANALYTICAL AND CRITICAL
STUDIES OF THE WRITERS

WITH INTRODUCTIONS
AND NOTES

BY

ARTHUR B. SIMONDS, A.M.

*Fellow in the Romance Languages
at Columbia College*

G. P. PUTNAM'S SONS

NEW YORK
27 West Twenty-third Street.

LONDON
24 Bedford Street, Strand.

The Knickerbocker Press

1894

Electrotyped, Printed and Bound by
The Knickerbocker Press, New York
G. P. PUTNAM'S SONS

What is a Poet? He is a man speaking to men: a man endowed with more lively sensibility, more enthusiasm and tenderness, who has a greater knowledge of human nature, and a more comprehensive soul, than are supposed to be common among mankind.

WORDSWORTH'S *"Preface to Lyrical Ballads."*

PREFACE.

The present volume has two distinct aims. It includes, first, a compilation of American poems (mostly short selections) drawn from the era beginning about the commencement of the century and reaching to the present day. As a compilation, therefore, it may be of interest to the general reader, as well as of special service to a student of literature wishing to acquaint himself readily with types of American poetry.

Secondly, the book may, it is hoped, be useful for making an inductive study, both of the chief American poets and, less completely, of the other poets from whose writings extracts are taken according to the plan of the volume. The order in critical study should be, first, the single poem; then the poems of one author, later the poetry of this author's period; finally, the consideration of American poetry as a whole. Thus Bryant's composition, *Thanatopsis*, is first to be studied, then, by means of successive examination of other poems, a view is to be gained of the whole of Bryant's verse. After Bryant, with increasing attention to the comparison of an author's poems one with another, Whittier, Emerson, and the other poets of the same group may be studied in a similar way; and the successive inductions collated and compared to show the poetical worth, as a group, of these "Classics." Around this group may then be viewed and with it compared, after similar but more brief special study, the other groups. At the close, therefore, of such an examination, the student should be prepared to arrive at a just estimate of American poetry in its intimate relations!

The teacher or the student, who wishes to make his study more thorough, may employ the volume not merely as a *text*, but as a *hand-book* introductory to a careful private reading of the best books on the special fields of the subject. For this purpose, in connection with the introductory sketch to each principal poet, selected bibliographical references are given, directing attention to the works which have seemed to the editor the most effective for rendering each author's personality clear and vivid. Among such references, the editions recommended of the poems may be assumed as first in importance; then the biographies of the poet; lastly his prose works. In the bibliographies, which have been made purposely brief, magazine articles on the poets have not been given mention. Such articles may, in certain cases, undoubtedly be of service, but dealing as they usually do with complex questions rather than with elementary matters, they need to be used, in the case of beginners, with extreme caution, and should hardly ever be regarded either as authoritative in themselves, or as worthy of complete acceptance for moulding the opinions of any student who has not finished the preliminary groundwork. Good cyclopedias, however, will often be found convenient for giving in a brief space the facts of an author's life. In general, the largest public libraries may of course, be used to advantage by students within reach of them.

For showing, as a further step, the place of poetry as a part of American thought and literature, Richardson's *American Literature* (G. P. Putnam's Sons) will be found a trustworthy guide.

But even without the opportunities afforded by helps, like these, good work may be done by means of a private collection composed of the works indicated. More valuable, however, than anything else is careful choice and attention in respect to what is noble in the spirit of poetry itself.

The contents have been divided, also for didactic reasons, into two parts; and on the same ground, these parts are further subdivided. In Part I. authors who (with one exception) are no longer living are represented by several poems, and are considered more fully than are the authors in Part II. In the first group, under Part I. are included the authors who, in the general opinion (perhaps in one or two instances in the opinion held by the editor), stand in the front rank; in the second group are selections from certain other prominent poets who died not long ago. Part II. is made up of poems by other authors, with brief notices prefixed in each case: a plan intended to prevent total ignorance on the part of the student of the writers of the great mass of

American poetry, as well as to avoid pronouncing to
an unnecessary degree upon the importance of the
earlier authors partly forgotten or of contemporary
poets who still have a future in which to produce.

Of the subdivisions of Part II., the collection of
war-ballads, grouped in subdivision II., explains itself. Between subdivisions I., and III., the following
tentative line of demarcation was drawn : poets born
before 1820 were placed in subdivision I.; those
after 1820 in subdivision III. While such classifica-
tion may appear somewhat arbitrary, it was adopted
as a preliminary toward indicating that decided
differences exist between early and later American
verse. Most of these differences may be more easily
felt than defined. One of the principal distinc-
tions is perhaps that the former tended to rudeness,
the latter to refinement of form.

Some exceptions have been made. Certain authors,
for instance, who were born before 1820 but who are
still living or whose works are comparatively recent,
are classed as " Contemporaries."

In taking up the present book for study, the
group " Classics," which is placed first, will be found
as a rule the most convenient to begin upon ; but in
this group it may be desirable to omit Poe and
Very,[1] if the book is used for younger classes. *At
Swords' Points* may be taken, without previous

---

[1] The reasons for the insertion of the poetry of Jones Very in the
division entitled " Classics " are given in the separate introduction to
Very's poems. That one purpose of the volume is to be useful to
readers who are somewhat mature, makes the innovation no indis-
cretion at most. My reservation, as in regard to Poe, would suggest
the limitation of the experiment.

study, for reading aloud, or for recitation. For purposes of literary study, however, this group as well as the remaining three can to advantage be preceded by "Classics"; while the last group in Part I., and the last in Part II. had better not be studied critically in class except by the most mature.

In the course of the study of American poetry, a treatise on the general subject of poetry, such as Bryant's *Lectures on Poetry* (found in the first volume of his prose writings), or Wordsworth's *Preface to the Lyrical Ballads*, can be read to advantage.

After the native field has been thoroughly gone over, a modest estimate of the results secured may follow a reading of Leigh Hunt's discussion, "*An Answer to the Question 'What is Poetry?'*" A patriotic reader will do well to remember, that as Mr. Richardson has finely said, "Though thought cannot die, the life of books and of authors is of minor importance."

Acknowledgment must be made to those publishers or others whose courtesy in granting the use of copyrighted material has made this volume possible. Those to whom I am indebted, and the volumes from which the respective works are taken (or the poems themselves), are as follows:

Messrs. HOUGHTON, MIFFLIN, & Co.:

T. B. Aldrich's Poems,

Mrs. Elizabeth Akers Allen's *The Silver Bridge and Other Poems*,

Alice and Phœbe Cary's Poems,

Miss Cone's *Oberon and Puck*, and *The Ride to the Lady and Other Poems*,

Cranch's *The Bird and the Bell*, and *Caliban*.

Emerson's Poems, and *May-Day and Other Pieces*,
Bret Harte's Poetical Works,
Holmes's Poems,
Lucy Larcom's Poems,
Longfellow's Poems,
Lowell's Poetical Works and *Heartease and Rue*
Parson's Poems,
Saxe's Poems,
Sill's Poems,
Stedman's Poems,
Story's Poems,
Taylor's Poems,
Celia Thaxter's Poems,
Edith Thomas's *Lyrics and Sonnets, A New Year's Masque,*
  and *Round the Year*,[1]
Thoreau's *The Fishing Boy*,
Whittier's Poetical Works,
Woodberry's *North-Shore Watch, and Other Poems*,

Messrs. D. APPLETON & CO.:
Bryant's Poems,
Halleck's Poems,
Songs and Ballads of the Civil War,
Songs and Ballads of the Revolution.

Messrs. A. C. ARMSTRONG & SON:
Poe's Poetical Works.[2]

THE BALTIMORE PUBLISHING CO.:
Ryan's *The Conquered Banner.*

THE BOWEN-MERRILL CO., of Indianapolis:
Riley's *Old-Fashioned Roses.*

---

[1] In a few instances, as with this author, the titles of other volumes than those used for purposes of selection have been given.

[2] I take pleasure in quoting from the letter of this firm: "We write to give you the permission you ask for, provided you will name us as publishers and sole owners of all of Poe's works, and so state our firm name and address.   Yours respectfully,
                    "A. C. ARMSTRONG & SON,
                            "New York."

THE CASSELL PUBLISHING CO.:
Miss Gilmore's *Pipes from the Prairies*,
O'Reilly's Poems.[1]

Messrs. EFFINGHAM, MAYNARD & CO.:
Willis's Poems.

Messrs. LEE & SHEPARD:
Mrs. Howe's *Battle Hymn of the Republic.*

THE J. B. LIPPINCOTT CO.:
Read's Poetical Works.

Messrs. LONGMANS, GREEN, & CO.:
Higginson's *Madonna di San Sisto.*

THE D. LOTHROP CO.:
Hayne's Poems,
Scollard's *With Reed and Lyre.*

Mr. GEORGE GOTTSBERGER PECK:
Mrs. Cooke's Poems.

Messrs. G. P. PUTNAM'S SONS:
American War Ballads, compiled by G. C. Eggleston,
Elaine and Dora Read Goodale's *Apple Blossoms, In Berk-
shire with the Wild Flowers, Verses from Sky Farm, All
Round the Year.*
J. H. Morse's *Summer-Haven Songs.*

Messrs. ROBERTS BROTHERS:
Verses by (H. H.), Mrs. Jackson.

Messrs. CHARLES SCRIBNER'S SONS:
Lanier's Poems,
Lathrop's *Dreams and Days.*

THE F. A. STOKES CO.:
Cheney's *Wood-Blooms* and *Thistle Drift.*

Dr. R. M. BUCKE:
Whitman's November Boughs and Leaves of Grass.

Mrs. J. T. FIELDS:
Fields's *The Stars and Stripes.*

---

[1] A volume of extracts from O'Reilly's Poems, entitled *Watch-
words*, is published by the Cupples Co., Boston.

Mr. C. II. (JOAQUIN) MILLER :
In Classic Shades,
Songs of Italy,
Songs of the Sierras,
Songs of the Sunlands.

Mr. YVON PIKE :
Dixie and *Every Year.*

Mr. R. II. STODDARD :
The Country Life.

Miss L. L. A. VERY :
Jones Very's Poems.

Among those to whom, in the preparation of this volume, I have been indebted for personal kindness and advice, I desire to express my thanks to Mr. John Vance Cheney, to Mr. C. F. Holder, and to Mr. D. C. Lockwood ; to Prof. C. M. Gayley ; and especially to Prof. H. A. Todd. To my former fellow-teacher, Mr. Austin Lewis, I wish to make acknowledgment for valuable suggestions. Among the books consulted, I have to refer to the Appendix by Mr. Arthur Stedman to the *Library of American Literature,* to which I have frequently resorted for facts about authors' lives.

In conclusion, I would crave the indulgence of those who, I am fully aware, know much more about poetry than I. They will see the defects of my performance, but they will also appreciate what difficulties have attended the task. If my volume may succeed in winning from them acceptance as a deserving attempt in the right direction, I shall feel well repaid for the labor of its preparation.

A. B. S.

PARIS, France, *October, 1894.*

CONTENTS

xiii

Contents.

II.—PRE-EMINENT LATER WRITERS.

Contents.

PART II.

I.—FORERUNNERS.

II—AT SWORDS' POINTS.

Contents.

III.—CONTEMPORARIES.

Contents.

Contents.

AMERICAN SONG

AMERICAN SONG.

PART I.

1. Classics.

THE works of writers whose thoughts, whose words, and whose memories are vital for successive generations, are those to whom is permitted the name of *Classics*. It was by writers of this class that American literature, in the deeper sense of the term, was begun ; literature which, intelligently studied, should form an important part of the education of every American boy and girl.[1]

This group, distinguished for breadth both of culture and of character, was not limited, in the source of its inspiration, to America. Among the influences due to the poetry of foreign lands, the principal influence came from that vigorous poetry of England which sprang up about the beginning of the nineteenth century. An account, for purposes of brief study, of the origin of this American poetry,

---

[1] A perfect American culture will include also the prose works of Emerson and Hawthorne.

need, therefore, not go back to the epoch of the first settlements; but requires only to mention the adoption of style from English literature and from other literatures, and may then proceed to mark the poetic achievements, under American conditions, according to the laws of poetic truth and poetic beauty.

From this point of view, if we include the field of literature as a whole, the first man of letters in America was Washington Irving. A man of taste and feeling, who was familiar with the social conditions of both sides of the Atlantic, Irving prepared the way for the wide development of American literature not only through his expression of cosmopolitan ideas, but also by awakening a public sentiment for literature of a higher kind than had been before realized ; and thus more easily, after Irving, arose a number of writers, who, in prose or poetry, gave themselves generously to their art.

Before this general result, however, and only a little after the beginning of Irving's career, the solitary figure of Bryant had stood forth as a poet worthy of high honor as a writer of English verse. It may be noted in passing that American literature in Bryant goes back, therefore, a score of years before Tennyson had printed a line, and has, at the present time, accordingly, an element of age as well as of apparent permanence.

In the decades following Bryant's first publication, literature as a profession being more favored through the springing up in the community of an interest in books of an æsthetic description, the poetic product became larger and richer. In purpose, as in character, this poetry was somewhat varied. Sometimes, as in the verses of Whittier and Lowell, the cause of anti-slavery was contended for; with other writers, such as Longfellow and Poe, the poetry appealed chiefly to the imagination.

The group as a whole is the part of American poetry, as has been said, which should at the present time be most studied. Forerunners of it are of less importance as literature, and later verse is the work of writers of to-day, who, being contemporary and having the possibility of a poetic future, cannot fairly be criticised in the same way as those whose work stands as done.

One certain word of praise may be passed on the group now under consideration. In general, perhaps, they did not write too much; what they did write they wrote as well as they could. In their work, also, in keeping and in enlarging both poetic and spiritual laws, they are in this country historic.

WILLIAM CULLEN BRYANT.

William Cullen Bryant was born November 3, 1794, at Cummington, a village situated beautifully among the Berkshire Hills of Massachusetts. From the Bryant as well as from the maternal side, he inherited strong poetical tastes. His father owning a library of seven hundred volumes, and having excellent literary judgment, Cullen, as he was called, was carefully trained in writing verse. At first he was taught to imitate the English poets of the eighteenth century, especially Pope ; later he studied Wordsworth, from whom he learned to observe nature and to think poetically. Not long after acquiring acquaintance with the *Lyrical Ballads*[1] and with the Greek poets, Bryant, who had attended college a single year, wrote his first draft of *Thanatopsis*.

The fundamental conception of the poem—the earth as a vast sepulchre—occurred to him during a ramble in the summer of 1811. We are fortunate in knowing something of its process of creation. Reflecting how all who live, himself included, must die, he began in the middle of a line :

---

[1] By Wordsworth and Coleridge.

4

" Yet a few days, and thee
   The all-beholding sun shall see no more
   In all his course ; "

and ended with the words :

" And make their bed with thee."

He afterward added his cheerful introduction and
the majestic, impressive conclusion.[1] A piece somewhat similar, *The Inscription for the Entrance to a
Wood*, written four years later, and published originally under the title of *A Fragment*, proclaimed for
the first time in America[2] the quiet happiness of
nature as open and communicable to men.

   To a Waterfowl, in the same year, is a contemplation far more sublime and profound in conception.[3]
From the self-consciousness of *Thanatopsis* and the
Inscription, the poet attains, at the same time with
higher art, a wider, truer view. His faith, as he says
in the first stanza, has brought him peace.

   Of similar calmness, *A Winter-Piece*,[4] in 1820, con-
trasting with the summer scenes of the *Inscription*,
delicately suggests sights minutely observed and
adorned richly with fancy.

   Inspired also in 1820, *Oh, Fairest of the Rural
Maids*, exquisitely ideal in its borrowings from nature, is a noble tribute to Bryant's lady-love. How

[1] A good example of the process of imaginative conception.

[2] It was written before the latter part of *Thanatopsis*.

[3] See the account of the composition of this poem in Godwin's *Life
of Bryant*.

[4] *Cf.* parts of Whittier's *Snow-Bound* and Lowell's *Vision of Sir
Launfal*, for similar description of winter scenes.

precious she was to him after marriage is told in the later poems, *The Future Life* and *The Life That Is*; how grief-stricken he was at her death is seen in *October, 1866*. Other poems, *The Hymn to Death*, *To ———*, *The Death of the Flowers*, and *The Past*, contain memories of his father and of his sister.

The Rivulet, dated Cummington, 1823, goes to make up, like the *Inscription*, the surroundings of Bryant's home; and is characterized by a tone of wise experience joined to sweet lyric freshness.[1] Written near the close of Bryant's ten years' practice of the law, the poem well represents that period of his poetic production: a time when his heart was given to poetry especially, and when his imagination was constantly expanding.[2]

In 1827, Bryant commenced his editorial duties with *The Evening Post*,[3] and continued them for the remainder of his life. *The Battle-field*, a poem in great degree personal, expresses the political earnestness underlying Bryant's chief object for the next thirty-five years. Still, he increased largely his poetic resource and variety. *The Damsel of Peru*, for instance, shows invention; and the *Two Graves*,[4] an individuality unique in theme and in details.

[1] Note also, on the artistic side, the melody of the poem.

[2] Not, however, with the vigor that Longfellow's was wont.

[3] As editor of *The Evening Post*, Bryant's services to journalism were no less wise and fearless than distinguished. See extracts in Godwin's *Life* and elsewhere. The matter and the manner of his editorials were weighty and matchless.

[4] *Cf.* here, and in connection with *Thanatopsis*, the fact that opposite Bryant's birthplace, on the upper side of the road, was a cemetery. The *Graves* were not here, however, but remote, in an obscure spot.

Again, the unpretentious poem, *The Fringed Gentian*, reflects the modest charm of the flower, and has a distinctive elegance of style. More difficult in performance, *Catterskill Falls* is aërially light in fancy. Poems of a larger horizon are the imaginative *Hunter's Vision* and *The Prairies*; with breadth, height is combined in the two kindred pieces, *The Firmament* and *When the Firmament Quivers with Daylight's Young Beam*. Of the rest, *O Mother of a Mighty Race* blends imagination with patriotic pride; *A Hymn of the Sea* is powerfully conceived; and spiritual truth infuses *The Land of Dreams* and *The Conqueror's Grave*.

Thirty Poems, in Bryant's seventieth year, is remarkable chiefly for containing political verse of vigor, together with gentler poems dealing with the mysterious region of fairy-land.

Among the pieces of this period, *Italy* exhibits Bryant's reach of sympathy at its widest. He was especially interested in Italian independence, and this confident burst of prophecy was followed about a decade later by his address on the attainment of Italian unity. Among poems on America, *Not Yet* is admirable for its energy and firmness; *The Death of Slavery*, full of passion and sublimity.

Of his lighter, more graceful product, the unfinished poem, *A Tale of Cloudland*, suggests an intention on his part of an extended treatment of the supernatural. *Sella*, a simple idyl, strange and wonderful, and *Little People of the Snow* are artistic stories for children; the former tinged with classic as well as modern color, the latter much resembling the German folk-lore.

A version of the fifth book of the *Odyssey* included in *Thirty Poems* led Bryant to undertake the whole of the *Odyssey* and the *Iliad*. As an English translation, Bryant's *Homer* is one of the best.

Another of the collection, *Waiting by the Gate*, portrays the grand equanimity of the sage as he muses on the approach of death. A still more universal song, almost terrible in its bold dealing with the fate of mankind, and irresistible in its sweep, is *The Flood of Years*, one of Bryant's last. Not long after this came his death, which occurred in New York, June 12, 1878.

Special references : Parke Godwin's editions of *Bryant's Poems* and of his *Prose Writings*, and Godwin's *Life of Bryant*—all published by Appleton.

THANATOPSIS.

To him who in the love of nature holds
Communion with her visible forms, she speaks
A various language ; for his gayer hours
She has a voice of gladness, and a smile
And eloquence of beauty, and she glides
Into his darker musings, with a mild
And healing sympathy, that steals away
Their sharpness ere he is aware.   When thoughts
Of the last bitter hour come like a blight
Over thy spirit, and sad images
Of the stern agony, and shroud, and pall,
And breathless darkness, and the narrow house,
Make thee to shudder, and grow sick at heart ;—

Go forth, under the open sky, and list
To Nature's teachings, while from all around—
Earth and her waters, and the depths of air,—
Comes a still voice.—Yet a few days, and thee
The all-beholding sun shall see no more
In all his course ; nor yet in the cold ground,
Where thy pale form was laid, with many tears,
Nor in the embrace of ocean, shall exist
Thy image.   Earth that nourished thee, shall claim
Thy growth, to be resolved to earth again,
And, lost each human trace, surrendering up
Thine individual being, shalt thou go
To mix forever with the elements,
To be a brother to the insensible rock
And to the sluggish clod, which the rude swain
Turns with his share, and treads upon.   The oak
Shall send his roots abroad, and pierce thy mould.
Yet not to thine eternal resting-place
Shalt thou retire alone—nor couldst thou wish
Couch more magnificent.   Thou shalt lie down
With patriarchs of the infant world—with kings,
The powerful of the earth—the wise, the good,
Fair forms, and hoary seers of ages past,
All in one mighty sepulchre.—The hills
Rock-ribbed and ancient as the sun,—the vales
Stretching in pensive quietness between ;
The venerable woods—rivers that move
In majesty, and the complaining brooks
That make the meadows green ; and, poured round all,
Old ocean's gray and melancholy waste,—
Are but the solemn decorations all
Of the great tomb of man.   The golden sun,
The planets, all the infinite host of heaven,
Are shining on the sad abodes of death,

Through the still lapse of ages.　All that tread
The globe are but a handful to the tribes
That slumber in its bosom.—Take the wings
Of morning—and the Barcan [1] desert pierce,
Or lose thyself in the continuous woods
Where rolls the Oregon, [2] and hears no sound,
Save his own dashings—yet—the dead are there ;
And millions in those solitudes, since first
The flight of years began, have laid them down
In their last sleep—the dead reign there alone.
So shalt thou rest—and what if thou withdraw
Unheeded by the living—and no friend
Take note of thy departure ?　All that breathe
Will share thy destiny.　The gay will laugh
When thou art gone, the solemn brood of care
Plod on, and each one as before will chase
His favorite phantom ; yet all these shall leave
Their mirth and their employments, and shall come
And make their bed with thee.　As the long train
Of ages glide away, the sons of men,
The youth in life's green spring, and he who goes
In the full strength of years, matron, and maid,
And the sweet babe, and the gray-headed man,—
Shall one by one be gathered to thy side,
By those, who in their turn shall follow them.
So live that when thy summons comes to join
The innumerable caravan, that moves
To that mysterious realm, where each shall take
His chamber in the silent halls of death,
Thou go not, like the quarry-slave at night,

[1] *Barca*, a maritime region of North Africa, forming the eastern division of Tripoli.
[2] *Oregon*, the Columbia River, which lies partly in Oregon.

Scourged to his dungeon, but, sustained and soothed
By an unfaltering trust, approach thy grave,
Like one who wraps the drapery of his couch
About him, and lies down to pleasant dreams.

INSCRIPTION FOR THE ENTRANCE TO A WOOD.

Stranger, if thou hast learned a truth which needs
No school of long experience, that the world
Is full of guilt and misery, and hast seen
Enough of all its sorrows, crimes, and cares,
To tire thee of it, enter this wild wood
And view the haunts of Nature. The calm shade
Shall bring a kindred calm, and the sweet breeze
That makes the green leaves dance, shall waft a balm
To thy sick heart. Thou wilt find nothing here
Of all that pained thee in the haunts of men
And made thee loathe thy life. The primal curse
Fell, it is true, upon the unsinning earth,
But not in vengeance. God hath yoked to Guilt
Her pale tormentor, Misery. Hence, these shades
Are still the abodes of gladness; the thick roof
Of green and stirring branches is alive
And musical with birds, that sing and sport
In wantonness of spirit; while below,
The squirrel, with raised paws and form erect,
Chirps merrily. Throngs of insects in the shade
Try their thin wings and dance in the warm beam
That waked them into life. Even the green trees
Partake the deep contentment; as they bend
To the soft winds, the sun from the blue sky
Looks in and sheds a blessing on the scene.

Scarce less the cleft-born wild-flower seems to enjoy
Existence, than the winged plunderer
That sucks its sweets.   The massy rocks themselves,
And the old and ponderous trunks of prostrate trees
That lead from knoll to knoll a causey rude
Or bridge the sunken brook, and their dark roots,
With all the earth upon them, twisting high,
Breathe fixed tranquillity.   The rivulet
Sends forth glad sounds, and tripping o'er its bed
Of pebbly sands, or leaping down the rocks,
Seems, with continuous laughter, to rejoice
In its own being.   Softly tread the marge,
Lest from her midway perch thou scare the wren
That dips her bill in water.   The cool wind,
That stirs the stream in play, shall come to thee,
Like one that loves thee nor will let thee pass
Ungreeted, and shall give its light embrace.

TO A WATERFOWL.

Whither, 'midst falling dew,
While glow the heavens with the last steps of day,
Far, through their rosy depths, dost thou pursue
Thy solitary way ?

Vainly the fowler's eye
Might mark thy distant flight to do thee wrong,
As, darkly seen against the crimson sky,
Thy figure floats along.

Seek'st thou the plashy brink
Of weedy lake, or marge of river wide,
Or where the rocky billows rise and sink
On the chafed ocean side ?

There is a Power whose care
Teaches thy way along that pathless coast,—
The desert and illimitable air,—
  Lone wandering, but not lost.

All day thy wings have fanned,
At that far height, the cold thin atmosphere,
Yet stoop not, weary, to the welcome land,
  Though the dark night is near.

And soon that toil shall end ;
Soon shalt thou find a summer home, and rest,
And scream among thy fellows ; reeds shall bend,
  Soon o'er thy sheltered nest.

Thou 'rt gone, the abyss of heaven
Hath swallowed up thy form ; yet, on my heart
Deeply hath sunk the lesson thou hast given,
  And shall not soon depart.

He who, from zone to zone,
Guides through the boundless sky thy certain flight,
In the long way that I must tread alone
  Will lead my steps aright.

A WINTER PIECE.

The time has been that these wild solitudes,
Yet beautiful as wild, were trod by me
Oftener than now ; and when the ills of life
Had chafed my spirit—when the unsteady pulse
Beat with strange flutterings—I would wander forth
And seek the woods. The sunshine on my path
Was to me as a friend. The swelling hills,

The quiet dells retiring far between,
With gentle invitation to explore
Their windings, were a calm society
That talked with me and soothed me.   Then the chant
Of birds, and chime of brooks, and soft caress
Of the fresh sylvan air, made me forget
The thoughts that broke my peace, and I began
To gather simples by the fountain's brink,
And lose myself in day-dreams.   While I stood
In Nature's loneliness, I was with one
With whom I early grew familiar, one
Who never had a frown for me, whose voice
Never rebuked me for the hours I stole
From cares I loved not, but of which the world
Deems highest, to converse with her.   When shrieked
The bleak November winds, and smote the woods,
And the brown fields were herbless, and the shades,
That met above the merry rivulet,
Were spoiled, I sought, I loved them still ; they seemed
Like old companions in adversity.
Still there was beauty in my walks ; the brook,
Bordered with sparkling frost-work, was as gay
As with its fringe of summer flowers.   Afar,
The village with its spires, the path of streams,
And dim receding valleys, hid before
By interposing trees, lay visible
Through the bare grove, and my familiar haunts
Seemed new to me.   Nor was I slow to come
Among them, when the clouds, from their still skirts,
Had shaken down on earth the feathery snow,
And all was white.   The pure keen air abroad,
Albeit it breathed no scent of herb, nor heard
Love-call of bird nor merry hum of bee,

Was not the air of death. Bright mosses crept
Over the spotted trunks, and the close buds,
That lay along the boughs, instinct with life,
Patient, and waiting the soft breath of Spring,
Feared not the piercing spirit of the North.
The snow-bird twittered on the beechen bough,
And 'neath the hemlock, whose thick branches bent
Beneath its bright cold burden, and kept dry
A circle on the earth, of withered leaves,
The partridge found a shelter. Through the snow
The rabbit sprang away. The lighter track
Of fox, and the raccoon's broad path were there,
Crossing each other. From his hollow tree,
The squirrel was abroad, gathering the nuts
Just fallen, that asked the winter cold and sway
Of winter blast, to shake them from their hold.
    But winter has yet brighter scenes,—he boasts
Splendors beyond what gorgeous Summer knows ;
Or Autumn, with his many fruits, and woods
All flushed with many hues. Come, when the rains
Have glazed the snow, and clothed the trees with ice ;
While the slant sun of February pours
Into the bowers a flood of light. Approach !
The incrusted surface shall upbear thy steps,
And the broad arching portals of the grove
Welcome thy entering. Look ! the massy trunks
Are cased in the pure crystal ; each light spray,
Nodding and tinkling in the breath of heaven,
Is studded with its trembling water-drops,
That stream with rainbow radiance as they move.
But round the parent stem the long low boughs
Bend, in a glittering ring, and arbors hide
The glassy floor. Oh ! you might deem the spot

The spacious cavern of some virgin mine,
Deep in the womb of earth—where the gems grow,
And diamonds put forth radiant rods and bud
With amethyst and topaz—and the place
Lit up, most royally, with the pure beam
That dwells in them.   Or happily the vast hall
Of fairy palace, that outlasts the night,
And fades not in the glory of the sun ;
Where crystal columns send forth slender shafts
And crossing arches ; and fantastic aisles
Wind from the sight in brightness, and are lost
Among the crowded pillars.   Raise thine eye,—
Thou seest no cavern roof, no palace vault ;
There the blue sky and the white drifting cloud
Look in.   Again, the wildered fancy dreams
Of spouting fountains, frozen as they rose,
And fixed, with all their branching jets, in air
And all their sluices sealed.   All, all is light ;
Light without shade.   But all shall pass away
With the next sun.   From numberless vast trunks,
Loosened, the crashing ice shall make a sound
Like the far roar of rivers, and the eve
Shall close o'er the brown woods as it was wont.
And it is pleasant, when the noisy streams
Are just set free, and milder suns melt off
The plashy snow, save only the firm drift
In the deep glen or the close shade of pines,—
'T is pleasant to behold the wreaths of smoke
Roll up among the maples of the hill,
Where the shrill sound of youthful voices wakes
The shriller echo, as the clear pure lymph,
That from the wounded trees, in twinkling drops,
Falls 'mid the golden brightness of the morn,

Is gathered in with brimming pails, and oft,
Wielded by sturdy hands, the stroke of axe
Makes the woods ring.   Along the quiet air,
Come and float calmly off the soft light clouds,
Such as you see in summer, and the winds
Scarce stir the branches.   Lodged in sunny cleft,
Where the cold breezes come not, blooms alone
The little wind-flower, whose just opened eye
Is blue as the spring heaven it gazes at—
Startling the loiterer in the naked groves
With unexpected beauty, for the time
Of blossoms and green leaves is yet afar.
And ere it comes, the encountering winds shall oft
Muster their wrath again, and rapid clouds
Shade heaven, and bounding on the frozen earth
Shall fall their volleyed stores, rounded like hail,
And white like snow, and the loud North [1] again
Shall buffet the vexed forests in his rage.

"OH FAIREST OF THE RURAL MAIDS."

Oh fairest of the rural maids !
Thy birth was in the forest shades ;
Green boughs, and glimpses of the sky,
Were all that met thy infant eye.

Thy sports, thy wanderings, when a child,
Were ever in the sylvan wild ;
And all the beauty of the place
Is in thy heart and on thy face.

[1] North, the north wind.

The twilight of the trees and rocks
Is in the light shade of thy locks ;
Thy step is as the wind, that weaves
Its playful way among the leaves.

Thy eyes are springs, in whose serene
And silent waters heaven is seen ;
Their lashes are the herbs that look
On their young figures in the brook.

The forest depths, by foot unpressed,
Are not more sinless than thy breast ;
The holy peace that fills the air
Of those calm solitudes, is there.

ITALY.

Voices from the mountain speak ;
　　Apennines to Alps reply ;
Vale to vale and peak to peak
　　Toss an old-remembered cry :
　　　　" Italy
　　　　Shall be free ! "
Such the mighty shout that fills
All the passes of the hills.

All the old Italian lakes
　　Quiver at that quickening word :
Como with a thrill awakes ;
　　Garda to her depths is stirred ;
　　'Mid the steeps
　　Where he sleeps,
Dreaming of the elder years,
Startled Thrasymenus hears.

Sweeping Arno, swelling Po,
   Murmur freedom to their meads.
Tiber swift and Liris slow
   Send strange whispers from their reeds
      " Italy
      Shall be free,"
Sing the glittering brooks that slide,
Toward the sea, from Etna's side.

Long ago was Gracchus slain ;
   Brutus perished long ago ;
Yet the living roots remain
   Whence the roots of greatness grow.
      Yet again
      God-like men,
Sprung from that heroic stem,
Call the land to rise with them.

They who haunt the swarming street,
   They who chase the mountain boar,
Or, where cliff and billow meet,
   Prune the vine, or pull the oar,
      With a stroke
      Break their yoke ;
Slaves but yester-eve were they—
Freemen with the dawning day.

Looking in his children's eyes,
   While his own with gladness flash,
" These," the Umbrian father cries,
   " Ne'er shall crouch beneath the lash !
      These shall ne'er
      Brook to wear
Chains whose cruel links are twined
Round the crushed and withering mind."

Monarchs ! ye whose armies stand
  Harnessed for the battle-field ;
Pause, and from the lifted hand
  Drop the bolts of war ye wield.
    Stand aloof
    While the proof
Of the people's might is given ;
Leave their kings to them and heaven.

Stand aloof and see the oppressed
  Chase the oppressor, pale with fear,
As the fresh winds of the west
  Blow the misty valleys clear.
    Stand and see
    Italy
Cast the gyves she wears no more
To the gulfs that steep her shore.

THE RIVULET.

This little rill that, from the springs
Of yonder grove, its current brings,
Plays on the slope awhile, and then
Goes prattling into groves again.
Oft to its warbling waters drew
My little feet, when life was new.
When woods in early green were dressed,
And from the chambers of the west
The warm breezes, travelling out,
Breathed the new scent of flowers about,
My truant steps from home would stray,
Upon its grassy side to play,
List the brown thrasher's vernal hymn,
And crop the violet on its brim,

With blooming cheek and open brow,
As young and gay, sweet rill, as thou.

And when the days of boyhood came,
And I had grown in love with fame,
Duly I sought thy banks, and tried
My first rude numbers by thy side.
Words cannot tell how bright and gay
The scenes of life before me lay.
Then glorious hopes, that now to speak
Would bring the blood into my cheek,
Passed o'er me ; and I wrote, on high,
A name I deemed should never die.

Years change thee not. Upon yon hill
The tall old maples, verdant still,
Yet tell, in grandeur of decay,
How swift the years have passed away,
Since first, a child, and half afraid,
I wandered in the forest shade.
Thou, ever joyous rivulet,
Dost dimple, leap, and prattle yet ;
And sporting with the sands that pave
The windings of thy silver wave,
And dancing to thy own wild chime,
Thou laughest at the lapse of time.
The same sweet sounds are in my ear
My early childhood loved to hear ;
As pure thy limpid waters run,
As bright they sparkle to the sun ;
As fresh and thick the bending ranks
Of herbs that line thy oozy banks ;
The violet there, in soft May dew,
Comes up, as modest and as blue ;

As green amid thy current's stress,
Floats the scarce-rooted watercress ;
And the brown ground-bird, in thy glen,
Still chirps as merrily as then.

Thou changest not—but I am changed,
Since first thy pleasant banks I ranged ;
And the grave stranger, come to see
The play-place of his infancy,
Has scarce a single trace of him
Who sported once upon thy brim.
The visions of my youth are past—
Too bright, too beautiful to last.
I 've tried the world—it wears no more
The coloring of romance it wore.
Yet well has nature kept the truth
She promised to my earliest youth.
The radiant beauty shed abroad
On all the glorious works of God,
Shows freshly, to my sobered eye,
Each charm it wore in days gone by.

A few brief years shall pass away,
And I, all trembling, weak, and gray,
Bowed to the earth, which waits to fold
My ashes in the embracing mould
(If haply the dark will of fate
Indulge my life so long a date),
May come for the last time to look
Upon my childhood's favorite brook.
Then dimly on my eye shall gleam
The sparkle of thy dancing stream ;
And faintly on my ear shall fall,
Thy prattling current's merry call ;

Yet shalt thou flow as glad and bright
As when thou met'st my infant sight.

And I shall sleep—and on thy side,
As ages after ages glide,
Children their early sports shall try,
And pass to hoary age and die.
But thou, unchanged from year to year,
Gayly shalt play and glitter here ;
Amid young flowers and tender grass
Thy endless infancy shall pass ;
And, singing down thy narrow glen,
Shalt mock the fading race of men.

JOHN GREENLEAF WHITTIER.

Whittier is not only interesting, like Bryant, for poems which belong to a world of imagination and fancy apart from actual life, but for verse which urges political reform. Throughout the history of the slavery conflict, he wrote passionately, arousing his countrymen to convictions of their responsibility.

On the 12th of December, 1807, John Greenleaf Whittier was born in a farm-house near Haverhill, Essex County, Massachusetts. His first poetical inspiration, if we except the Bible, came from Burns, whom he read at fourteen and imitated for a time. Having gained at twenty-one a brief, hard-earned schooling at Phillips Academy, Andover, and having studied the traditions of a native region rich in living legends, he was led by contemplation of English poets, especially Scott, to the invention of *Mogg Megone*, a narrative poem which was based on early New England lore, and which may be taken as representing the poet's transition to originality.

From the date of *Mogg Megone* until 1850 he wrote a number of exquisite short poems, quiet and gentle in tone, unpretentious and various in subject, and manifesting successive stages of growth in power of intellect and of expression. *The Fountain*, in 1837, has the very spirit of Whittier's native hills and valleys. A cooling breeze seems to blow around and about the poet's language, and the whole picture is fresh and genuine. Another poem of nature, *Hampton Beach*, is vivid in sketching, intense in abstraction, and profound in spiritual meditation. More modest in form but of equal power is *The Well of Loch Maree*. Among poems of human associations, the innocent tenderness in *Memories* between the person and himself is to Whittier a remembrance both pleasant and precious. *Raphael*, artistic in form and in judgment, has a high compass of thought and of imagination. Of similar elevation, *To my Friend on the Death of his Sister*, is a model in its appreciation and delicacy of condolence. Equally true and perfect in sincerity and conscious pride is *Our State*.

Whittier meanwhile began to sing in sterner strains. Against slavery, *A Summons* appealed to latent manliness, proclaiming the shame of cowardly inaction. Similar but more forcible, *To Faneuil Hall*, an unnoticed poem among Whittier's best, combines vigor of purpose with thorough scorn and tearful pathos. There is in it the ring of the voice and the stamp of the foot. Whittier's commanding nature was never more roused than in this poem, and he put into it all his imperious spirit. In *Brown of Ossawatomie*, on the other hand, is the gentler hope and trust in a peaceful solution of the nation's problem. A similar piece, *Ein' Feste Burg*,[1] shows Whitter's inspired hope and his patient watching during the war. *The Song*

---

[1] *Ein' Feste Burg*, a sure stronghold.

of the Negro Boatmen, in 1862, common, simple, and
in dialect, images the joy of jubilee and the new
confidence imparted to the slaves by freedom.
Written about the same time, *What the Birds Said*
has its poetic element surpassed by its spiritual light
of promise. All this group have passion ; they come
from a whole nature on fire. Some pieces of the
period are fiercer than is usually regarded compatible
with literary perfection ; others have the apparent
fault of prosiness. But on the whole they have
claims to estimation as poems of deep content and
uncontrived expression ; they are slightly, if at all,
defective on the artistic side ; and far from being
marred by haste or impulsiveness, their truth of in-
tuition, strength of conception, and courage of utterance are often supported by cogent reasoning.

Whittier's power of intellect is still more evident
in his ideal portraits ; for no ordinary mind could
have treated successfully even the fall of Webster.
The method in *Ichabod* is unique ; the unflinching
exposure, with the contrast of the orator's former
glory, is far more severe than unmixed condemnation.
Rantoul, a panegyric poem written in 1853, is typical
of Whittier's commemoration of friends faithful to
the cause he revered. The poem itself is proud and
stately, chaste in simplicity, and one of the noblest
songs of America. Its figure is haloed with spiritual
worth. What matter if, in comparison with this
ideal shape, the historic original were really as great
or not? The important thing to notice is that there
is great thought and great feeling in Whittier. The
lines to Charles Summer again are remarkable for

their grand imagery. Here as before, Whittier is
like a painter worshipping the old saints. Better
than any of his contemporaries, he could perceive
virtue in the heroes of his generation.

Whittier has also uttered strong religious convictions. *My Soul and I* is a candid self-inquiry of
motives. *The Wish of To-Day* acknowledges the
resignation of age. *The Meeting* is very wise in its
criticism of a superficial philosophy. Yet his religious poems are not poems of argument but poems
of faith; faith in nature, faith in the present, faith
in his fellows, faith in God.

Whittier gave most attention to literary form
after the year 1850. A particular charm of style
often accompanies henceforth each poem. Almost
simultaneously shine the radiance of *Eva* and the
gleam of romance of *Maud Muller*. The latter with
the especially swift and direct *Barbara Frietchie* and
the somewhat coarser *Skipper Ireson's Ride* have
kept their places as the best executed by Whittier
in ballad form, in which he excelled. Of the same
class, a strange story, *Norumbega*, is individually
told. Side by side with ballads flowed from his pen
touching reminiscences of the poet's childhood.
Noteworthy in *The Barefoot Boy* are its painting and
emotion at the beginning and end. *Telling the Bees*
is quaintly and skilfully related; *My Playmate* is half
regretful for a lost love of boyhood; and the
later poem, *In School Days*, a mirror of guileless feeling, is still another of a group unsurpassed in artless-
ness. The narrative is blended with the personal
element in *Snow-Bound* and in *The Tent on the Beach*.

Snow-Bound, one of the longest successful American poems, appeals to the sentiment of New England by its imagination of her life of seventy years ago. *The Tent on the Beach* has, among other merits, an introduction charmingly dreamy, with attractive sketches of the men of letters who are the interlocutors.

The two foregoing narratives are the works of Whittier fullest of color and of poetic art, and (especially *Snow-Bound*) the tasks of his prime. The pieces subsequent, however, to 1868 are also true and strong ; and this last period of his perhaps generally excels all the others in simplicity of style. The verses written in 1871 on *Chicago* show that matters even of recent interest may be poetical ; *How the Women Went from Dover*, though realistic, is sympathetic ; and *Abram Morrison* describes a canny figure, homely and picturesque.

Reality of outward life and the great spiritual facts of his country and time are the air and the sunshine in which Whittier grew. In his descriptive verse, call the scenes of his pages local if we will, they possess a generous variety of interest from their significance as relating to New England, that region to which America owes so much. Whittier's moral aim, too, if specialized, bears the rich fruits of concentration. To the virtuous who read him carefully he is neither provincial nor hard to understand. That his works are not more fully esteemed is, I believe, because of the reverence for his character. Men, seeing that the man is superior to his work, do not perceive the sterling qualities which his poetry itself has. They forget that virtue and art at their high-est points partake each of the other. As Whittier's heart and action were, so is his poetry. We may attend too much sometimes to writers as well as doers seeking to cultivate in us exotic refine-ments which are false to our nature. Whittier, not only in his practical record but in his works, tells us what active and healthful virtue really is.

Special reference : Whittier's Poetical Works, edition of 1888, with notes by the author. Houghton, Mifflin, & Co.

THE FOUNTAIN.

Traveller ! on thy journey toiling
   By the swift Powow,[1]
With the summer sunshine falling
   On thy heated brow,
Listen, while all else is still,
To the brooklet from the hill.

Wild and sweet the flowers are blowing
   By that streamlet's side,
And a greener verdure showing,
   Where its waters glide,
Down the hill-slope murmuring on,
Over root and mossy stone.

Where yon oak his broad arms flingeth
   O'er the sloping hill,
Beautiful and freshly springeth
   That soft-flowing rill,

[1] *Powow*, a tributary of the Merrimack River.

Through its dark roots wreathed and bare,
Gushing up to sun and air.

Brighter waters sparkled never
  In that magic well,
Of whose gift of life forever
  Ancient legends tell,
In the lonely desert wasted,
And by mortal lip untasted.

Waters which the proud Castilian [1]
  Sought with longing eyes,
Underneath the bright pavilion
  Of the Indian skies,
Where his forest pathway lay
Through the blooms of Florida.

Years ago a lonely stranger,
  With the dusky brow
Of the outcast forest-ranger,
  Crossed the swift Powow,
And betook him to the rill,
And the oak upon the hill.

O'er his face of moody sadness
  For an instant shone
Something like a gleam of gladness,
  As he stooped him down
To the fountain's grassy side
And his eager thirst supplied.

[1] *The proud Castilian.* " De Soto in the sixteenth century pene-
trated into the wilds of a new world in search of gold and the
fountain of perpetual youth."

With the oak its shadows throwing
  O'er his mossy seat,
And the cool sweet waters flowing
  Softly at his feet,
Closely by the fountain's rim
That lone Indian seated him.

Autumn's earliest frost had given
  To the woods below
Hues of beauty, such as heaven
  Lendeth to its bow ;
And the soft breeze from the west
Scarcely broke their dreamy rest.

Far behind was Ocean striving
  With its chains of sand ;
Southward sunny glimpses giving,
  'Twixt the swells of land,
Of its calm and silvery track,
Rolled the tranquil Merrimack.

Over village, wood, and meadow
  Gazed that stranger man
Sadly, till the twilight shadow
  Over all things ran,
Save where spire and westward pane
Flashed the sunset back again.

Gazing thus upon the dwelling
  Of his warrior sires,
Where no lingering trace was telling
  Of their wigwam fires,
Who the gloomy thoughts might know
Of that wandering child of woe ?

Naked lay, in sunshine glowing,
   Hills that once had stood
Down their sides the shadows throwing
   Of a mighty wood,
Where the deer his covert kept,
And the eagle's pinion swept !

Where the birch canoe had glided
   Down the swift Powow,
Dark and gloomy bridges strided
   Those clear waters now ;
And where once the beaver swam
Jarred the wheel and frowned the dam.

For the wood-bird's merry singing,
   And the hunter's cheer,
Iron clang and hammer's ringing
   Smote upon his ear ;
And the thick and sullen smoke
From the blackened forges broke.

Could it be his fathers ever
   Loved to linger here ?
These bare hills, this conquer'd river,—
   Could they hold them dear,
With their native loveliness
Tamed and tortured into this ?

Sadly as the shades of even
   Gathered o'er the hill,
While the western half of heaven
   Blushed with sunset still,
From the fountain's mossy seat
Turned the Indian's weary feet.

Year on year hath flown forever,
  But he came no more
To the hillside or the river
  Where he came before.
But the villager can tell
Of that strange man's visit well.

And the merry children, laden
  With their fruits or flowers,—
Roving boy and laughing maiden,
  In their school-day hours,
Love the simple tale to tell
Of the Indian and his well.

TO FANEUIL HALL.[1]

1844.

Men ! if manhood still ye claim,
  If the Northern pulse can thrill,
Roused by wrong or stung by shame,
  Freely, strongly still ;
Let the sounds of traffic die :
  Shut the mill-gate—leave the stall,
Fling the axe and hammer by ;
  Throng to Faneuil Hall !

Wrongs which freemen never brooked,
  Dangers grim and fierce as they,
Which, like couching lions, looked
  On your fathers' way ;

[1] *Faneuil Hall*, in Boston, sometimes called the "Cradle of
Liberty."

3

These your instant zeal demand,
  Shaking with their earthquake call
Every rood of Pilgrim land—
  Ho, to Faneuil Hall !

From your capes and sandy bars,
  From your mountain ridges cold,
Through whose pines the westering stars
  Stoop their crowns of gold—
Come, and with your footsteps wake
  Echoes from that holy wall ;
Once again, for Freedom's sake,
  Rock your fathers' hall !

Up, and tread beneath your feet
  Every cord by party spun ;
Let your hearts together beat
  As the heart of one.
Banks and tariffs, stocks and trade,
  Let them rise or let them fall :
Freedom asks your common aid,—
  Up to Faneuil Hall !

Up, and let each voice that speaks,
  Ring from thence to Southern plains,
Sharply as the blow which breaks
  Prison-bolts and chains !
Speak as well becomes the free—
  Dreaded more than steel or ball,
Shall your calmest utterance be,
  Heard from Faneuil Hall !

Have they wronged us ? Let us then
  Render back nor threats nor prayers ;

Have they chained our free-born men?
  Let us unchain theirs!
Up! your banner leads the van,
  Blazoned "Liberty for all!"
Finish what your sires began!
  Up, to Faneuil Hall!

RANTOUL.[1]

One day, along the electric wire
  His manly word for Freedom sped;
We came next morn; that tongue of fire
  Said only, "He who spake is dead!"

Dead! while his voice was living yet,
  In echoes round the pillared dome!
Dead! while his blotted page lay wet
  With themes of state and loves of home!

Dead! in that crowning grace of time,
  That triumph of life's zenith hour!
Dead! while we watched his manhood's prime
  Break from the slow bud into flower!

Dead! he so great, and strong, and wise,
  While the mean thousands yet drew breath;
How deepened, through that dread surprise,
  The mystery and the awe of death!

From the high place whereon our votes
  Had borne him, clear, calm, earnest, fell
His first words, like the prelude notes
  Of some great anthem yet to swell.

[1] *Robert Rantoul,* born at Beverly, Mass., in 1805.

We seemed to see our flag unfurled,
  Our champion waiting in his place
For the last battle of the world—
  The Armageddon [1] of the race.

Through him we hoped to speak the word
  Which wins the freedom of the land ;
And lift, for human right, the sword
  Which dropped from Hampden's [2] dying hand.

For he had sat at Sidney's [3] feet,
  And walked with Pym [4] and Vane [5] apart ;
And through the centuries, felt the beat
  Of Freedom's march in Cromwell's [6] heart.

He knew the paths the worthies held,
  Where England's best and wisest trod ;
And, lingering, drank the springs that welled
  Beneath the touch of Milton's rod.

No wild enthusiast of the right,
  Self-poised and clear, he showed alway
The coolness of his northern night,
  The ripe repose of autumn's day.

---

[1] *Armageddon*, a region of Palestine.   See *Rev.* xvi., 14-16.

[2] *John Hampden*, an illustrious English patriot and statesman, born at London in 1594.

[3] *Sir Philip Sidney*, born at Penshurst, England, in 1554.

[4] *John Pym*, a wise associate of Hampden, born at Brymore, England, in 1554.

[5] *Sir Henry Vane*, an English statesman, born in Kent in 1589.

[6] *Oliver Cromwell*, Protector of England, born at Huntingdon in 1599.

His steps were slow, yet forward still
   He pressed where others paused or failed ;
The calm star clomb[1] with constant will,
   The restless meteor flashed and paled !

Skilled in its subtlest wile, he knew
   And owned the higher ends of Law ;
Still rose majestic on his view
   The awful Shape the schoolman saw.

Her home the heart of God ; her voice
   The choral harmonies whereby
The stars, through all their spheres, rejoice,
   The rhythmic rule of earth and sky !

We saw his great powers misapplied
   To poor ambitions ; yet, through all,
We saw him take the weaker side,
   And right the wronged, and free the thrall.

Now, looking o'er the frozen North
   For one like him in word and act,
To call her old, free spirit forth,
   And give her faith the life of fact,—

To break her party bonds of shame,
   And labor with the zeal of him
To make the Democratic name
   Of Liberty the synonym,—

[1] *Clomb*, past of climb ; not good in prose.

We sweep the land from hill to strand,
   We seek the strong, the wise, the brave,
And, sad of heart, return to stand
   In silence by a new-made grave !

There, where his breezy hills of home
   Look out upon his sail-white seas,
The sounds of winds and waters come,
   And shape themselves to words like these :

" Why, murmuring, mourn that he, whose power
   Was lent to Party over long,
Heard the still whisper at the hour
   He set his foot on Party wrong?

" The human life that closed so well
   No lapse of folly now can stain ;
The lips whence Freedom's protest fell
   No meaner thought can now profane.

" Mightier than living voice his grave
   That lofty protest utters o'er ;
Through roaring wind and smiting wave
   It speaks his hate of wrong once more.

" Men of the North ! your weak regret
   Is wasted here ; arise and pay
To freedom and to him your debt,
   By following where he led the way ! "

RALPH WALDO EMERSON.

The poetry of Emerson is to most persons hard to understand ; certainly so under conditions of mere surface reading. Yet, to understand it, takes a method neither long nor difficult. Two things only are requisite. To know Emerson's biography is indispensable ; and as appreciation of prose is easier than that of poetry and prepares the way for the latter, a reader, to discriminate in and to understand these poems, should acquaint himself with Emerson's essays.

Originally written and delivered as lectures, Emerson's prose writings find a counterpart in the well-known poems written to be recited, such as the *Concord Hymn*, the *Concord Ode*, and the *Boston Hymn*, which, being composed rhetorically, are not Emerson's best poems. The contemplative poem, *Voluntaries*, on the other hand, making universal application of a public subject, is indisputably of a high order. The idea of a just destiny behind the state is here expounded with the spiritual force that Emerson so much aspired to wield.

Other poems of Emerson's are autobiographical, sketching, as will be seen later, his inner history.

Outwardly his life was in the main quiet and uneventful. Ralph Waldo Emerson was born in Boston, May 25, 1803, on Summer Street, then in a suburban district. His ancestry included several New England ministers of more or less eminence. From earliest boyhood Emerson grew up under influence favorable to study. Morally he was constantly and strongly influenced by his aunt, Miss Mary Emerson, a serious woman, thoughtfully interested in her nephew. In 1817 Emerson entered Harvard College, where he seems not to have been remarkable in general as a scholar, and only barely so in composition. Yet he read (more for himself than for his professors) a good deal in the literature not only of the day but of earlier times. After graduation he taught for a number of years and later preached, resigning his charge in 1832 and sailing for Europe, where he remained about a year. On his return he began his lecturing, and from 1835 resided in Concord until his death, April 27, 1882.

As illustrating Emerson's biography, *Good-bye*, *Proud World*, *Berrying*, and *Terminus* are of slight and incidental value. The poet as a lover writes *To Ellen*, *To Eva*, *The Amulet*, and *Thine Eyes Still Shined*. Only sad, serious subjects, however, called out his richest, fullest power, as in the *Dirge* and *Threnody*. The development of his character as a whole is reflected in other poems, also in his journal and in his letters. All these data are valuable as showing the stages of growth in the mind of a man of letters. In his attitude towards himself, at twenty-one, he shows an inquiring spirit, a consciousness of his own defects, and a distrust of his ability. Next, in the series of little pieces entitled *Nature and Life*, and constituting a further deliberation, he begins consciously high resolve and advances toward nobler and nobler self-possession. The course of these years is one of the most beautiful tales, though fragmentary, of the spiritualizing of a soul. Afterwards, in his voyage to Europe, his notes at sea are in a new style, the lightness and the loveliness of his prose beginning to come forth. Europe gave him more than it gives to many; if it did not furnish Emerson's inspiration, it prepared him to receive it.

Not long after his return Emerson wrote the greater part of his poems and essays, and then it was that the woods and waters of New England began to supply him with his imagery and embellishments. Indeed, it is almost necessary to be a New Englander in order to understand him ; and to New Englanders his poems on nature have appealed strongly. He combines the sharp observation of the naturalist with the reverie of the artist and the idealist. His love of nature increasing as he grew older, he wrote more and with greater pains in this direction. The poem, *May-Day*, has parts in it in which Emerson is almost as attentive to finish of style as Milton is in his *Comus*. Both in Emerson's first and in his second volume hardly a poem on nature can be found but has its distinct excellence of sentiment or description. The melody of the *Humble-Bee*, the dainty picture of the *Titmouse*, the grandeur and the terraces of *Seashore*, and *Monadnoc*, the airy citadel, are not unusually striking by their variety of difference. Occasionally Emerson showed second sight, as when Musketaquid [1] symbolizes to him the vast, endless river of the ages. He is not so much at home, as in nature, in worldly themes, where the *Romany Girl*, with her wild gypsy grace, is almost his only representative.

Emerson's philosophical poems aim to exhibit intellectual and moral truths. Underlying each poem and often more suggested than expounded, a single idea is given, not abstractly, as with most philosophers, but bodied forth by a number of examples. The subjects are taken from fields widely distant in time and space. As if collecting material for experimenting in the New World, Emerson has drawn alike from the moderns, from the classics, and from the literature of the East. The subject may be a virtue (Heroism), an idea with a moral bearing (Nemesis), or even an association at bottom pagan (Brahma).

It is a question whether this poetry should be judged by a criterion applied commonly at present: that is, whether excellence here is dependent on the presence of matter " simple, sensuous, impassioned." [2] A poem filled with the kind of philosophy that Emerson treats of cannot perhaps be as simple as most poetry is, and still pursue its end. For philosophy in any form is not easy to understand ; certainly not for one who is ignorant of its methods, and who is as indisposed to study them as most

[1] Musketaquid, a river of Concord.

[2] " Simple, sensuous, impassioned,"—Matthew Arnold quoting Milton.

readers of poetry are. Since, furthermore, Emerson's philosophical generalizations in verse, instead of being expanded throughout a large volume, are condensed within a small compass, it may not be reasonable to expect more than a moderate transfer of the matter to metric expression.

On the whole it may be doubted whether Emerson's poetry has been over-estimated. Without being ever perhaps a consummate artist throughout even a short poem, Emerson has abundant and various manifestation of the poetic spirit. This perceived, one has next to see the ground of his pre-eminence. His admirers are wont, and rightly, to point to the fanciful beauty in the opening lines of the *Ode at Concord*, to the picturesqueness of the *Rhodora*, or to the charm of the *Humble-Bee*: poems carrying a certain aroma of intellectual and emotional suggestiveness in single lines. Yet depth is more to a poet's credit than elegance, and the tone of a poem more than quotable extracts. The greater forces and qualities, I repeat, lie in such poems as have the grandeur of *Voluntaries*, or the indirect expression and personal passion of the *Threnody*: poems where there is real seriousness, real perception of the fundamental forces in the world and in man; and poems also which distinguish Emerson as him among our poets who most grows upon one at the second reading. Such an excellence can mean only one thing—that in certain respects he is the greatest American poet.

Special references: Emerson's Poems, and *May-Day and Other Pieces*; Cabot's *Memoir of Emerson*; Holmes's *Emerson*, " American Men of Letters " Series (the chapter on Emerson's poetry),— Houghton, Mifflin, & Co.

GIVE ALL TO LOVE.

Give all to love ;
Obey thy heart ;
Friends, kindred, days,
Estate, good-fame,
Plans, credit, and the muse,—
Nothing refuse.

'T is a brave master
Let it have scope ;
Follow it utterly,
Hope beyond hope ;
High and more high
It dives [1] into noon,

With wing unspent,
Untold intent ;
But it is a god,
Knows its own path
And the outlets of the sky.
It was never for the mean ;
It requireth courage stout.

Souls above doubt,
Valor unbending,
It will reward,—
They shall return
More than they were,
And ever ascending.

Leave all for love ;
Yet, hear me, yet,

[1] *Dives.* What is the meaning of the word here?

One word more thy heart behoved,
One pulse more of vain endeavor,—
Keep thee to-day,
To-morrow, forever,
Free as an Arab
Of thy beloved.

Cling with life to the maid,
But when the surprise,
First vague shadow of surmise
Flits across her bosom young,
Of a joy apart from thee,
Free be she, fancy-free;
Nor thou detain her vesture's hem,
Nor the palest rose she flung
From her summer diadem.

Though thou loved her as thyself,
As a self of purer clay,
Though her parting dims the day,
Stealing grace from all alive;
Heartily know,
When half-gods go,
The gods arrive.

CHARACTER.

The sun set, but set not his hope;
Stars rose; his faith was earlier up:
Fixed on the enormous galaxy,
Deeper and older seemed his eye;
And matched his sufferance sublime
The taciturnity of time.

He spoke, and words more soft than rain
Brought the age of gold again :
His action won such reverence sweet
As hid all measure of the feat.

HERI, HODIE, CRAS.[1]

Shines the last age, the next with hope is seen,
To-day slinks poorly off unmarked between ;
Future or past no richer secret folds,
O friendless present ! than thy bosom holds.

[1] *Heri, Hodie, Cras*, yesterday, to-day, to-morrow.

EDGAR ALLAN POE.

As the author of *The Raven* and the prose tales, Poe not only holds a permanent place in American literature, but is widely read in Europe, particularly by the French. Among other single poems by Poe, many are unique in conception and in art. That he showed unusual keenness while criticising contemporary literature may also be perceived.

Edgar Allan Poe was born in Boston, January 19, 1809. His mother was of distinguished talent on the stage. On his father's side Poe was a grandson of General David Poe, an ardent patriot in the Revolution. Both parents dying before he was three years old, he was adopted by a Mr. John Allan, who greatly indulged him during his boyhood, and who in 1816 placed Poe in school for five years at Stoke Newington, England, among antique and picturesque surroundings. The intricate construction of the house where Poe attended and the venerableness of the village are described in the author's tale, *William Wilson.* In 1822 he continued his education at Richmond, Virginia, seeing there for the first time his friend, Mrs. Stannard, who assumed in his mind the position of an ideal love, and in memory of whom he wrote the short poem *To Helen* beginning

"Helen, thy beauty is to me,"

and published in his third volume of verse. In 1826 he entered the University of Virginia, where he studied Greek, Latin, French, Italian, and Spanish, although more proficient in the second and the third.

The two periods of imitation and originality are well marked in Poe's poetic production. In the first period, *Tamerlane*, published in 1827, shows the influence of Byron; and *Al Aaraaf*, two years later, that of Moore. These and *Politian*, which appeared several years afterwards, are Poe's only long poems.

To the River ——, in the collection headed by *Al Aaraaf*, is clear and suggestive in its language, and gives sign of the power in the volume of 1831, in which appeared several poems in a form subsequently changed, such as *Israfel*, which in its tone of high confidence stands by itself among Poe's works; and *The Pæan*, which later became *Lenore* with its almost perfect lines—

"Let no bell toll;—lest her sweet soul,
    Amid its hallowed mirth,
Should catch the note as it doth float—
Unto a high estate far up within the Heaven;—
From grief and groan to a golden throne
    Beside the King of Heaven."

Poe was soon busied in editorial work in New

York, then in Philadelphia, and later at Richmond, where, May 16, 1836, he married his cousin, Virginia Clemm.

During this period his poems were published singly. In *The Conqueror Worm*, Poe is not merely sombre, but tragic. *The Raven*, if not the most admirable, is the most celebrated American poem. While others of their creator's works are strongly marked by compression and individuality, *The Raven* has these to a surpassing degree. It has also the fineness of rhythm of *The Bells*, the weirdness of *The City by the Sea*, *The Haunted Palace*, or the tales, the beauty of the succeeding lyrics, and vividness, composition, and elegance of its own.

In the period reaching from the death of Mrs. Poe, January 30, 1847, till his own death, October 7, 1849, Poe produced several of his best poems. He seems here to have increased the progress towards sincerity with which poetically he proceeded all through life. *Eulalie* is a picture of his affection for his wife; *To My Mother*, an expression of his debt to Mrs. Clemm, his wife's mother. *The Bells*, on the other hand, is an exhibition of technical skill in versification. Among the rest, *To Helen*, addressed to Mrs. Whitman, and beginning

"I saw thee once—once only—years ago—"

is in fancy and high-strung emotion one of the highest points ever attained by Poe, a poem in which the least mistake or insincerity would have made it a failure. The incident described is said to have had

4

its foundation in his having seen her walking in the moonlight among the roses of her garden.

It is right and it is time to throw a veil over Poe's faults. As to his virtues, he was strongest on the intellectual side. Not only was his patience in literary labor of immense value to himself in his art, but his fearlessness in criticism has been a service to American literature.

To appreciate Poe, the imagination requires either distance of time or independence of attitude. It may, however, be observed that the interest attaching to his poetry is strictly of the personal and private kind. Yet if apart from *The Raven*, Poe was the least of the greater American poets, except as to form, in which he was careful exceedingly, who would affirm that in his originality as well as in clearness and execution he was inferior to any particular poet who wrote later?

Poe's tales are, among short prose works, at the head of American fiction ; and are inferior only to the more sustained romances of Hawthorne. In his essays Poe is best as a critic of poetry. He did not excel as a philosophical theorist ; for he had neither the kind of genius nor the training requisite. But it is well to note the frequent agreement between his *obiter dicta* when he gave critical judgments on literature and the views in Mr. Stedman's excellent *Poets of America*; and also to test Poe's conclusions by attentive study of the authors he criticised. Among the numerous examples of Poe's correctness are his brief characterization of Bryant's *Waterfowl* ; the comparison between Bryant and Longfellow, with the general criticism on other authors that suggests itself ; and again the enthusiastic comment upon Hawthorne.

For a view of Poe from all sides, in addition to Mr. Stedman's chapter on Poe in the *Poets of America*, for the literary aspect Lowell's powerfully analytical essay, prefixed to the complete authorized edition of Poe's works, ought to be read ; and for the biography several books in the case of this author. For the facts, Woodberry's Life of Poe (Houghton, Mifflin, & Co.), a work of special research, is the best. Ingram's is also worth reading, as giving the more favorable side of Poe's character ; or Gill's, but this, while it has a table of contents, is not indexed.

TO THE RIVER ——.

Fair river ! in thy bright, clear flow
   Of crystal, wandering water,
Thou art an emblem of the glow
   Of beauty—the unhidden heart—
   The playful magazines of art
In old Alberto's daughter ;

But when within thy wave she looks—
   Which glistens then, and trembles—
Why, then, the prettiest of brooks
   Her worshipper resembles ;
   For in his heart, as in thy stream,
      Her image deeply lies—
His heart which trembles at the beams
      Of her soul-searching eyes.

LENORE.

Ah, broken is the golden bowl ! the spirit flown forever !
Let the bell toll ! a saintly soul floats on the Stygian
river ;
And, Guy De Vere, hast thou no tear ?—weep now or
never more !
See ! on yon drear and rigid bier low lies thy love
Lenore !
Come ! let the burial rite be read—the funeral song be
sung !—
An anthem for the queenliest dead that ever died so
young—
A dirge for her the doubly dead in that she died so
young.

"Wretches ! ye loved her for her wealth and hated her
for her pride,
And when she fell in feeble health, ye blessed her that
she died !
How shall the ritual, then, be read ?—the requiem how
be sung
By you—by yours, the evil eye,—by yours, the slanderous
tongue,
That did to death the innocence that died, and died so
young ?

"*Peccavimus ;* but rave not thus ! and let a Sabbath song
Go up to God so solemnly the dead may feel no wrong !
The sweet Lenore hath 'gone before,' with Hope, that
flew beside,
Leaving thee wild for the dear child that should have
been thy bride—
For her, the fair and *débonnaire*, that now so lowly lies,

The life upon her yellow hair but not within her eyes—
The life still there, upon her hair—the death upon her
    eyes.

"Avaunt ! to-night my heart is light. No dirge will I
    upraise,
But waft the angel on her flight with a Pæan of old days !
Let no bell toll ! lest her sweet soul, amid its hallowed
    mirth,
Should catch the note, as it doth float up from the
    damned earth,
To friends above, from fiends below, the indignant ghost
    is riven—
From hell unto a high estate far up within the Heaven—
From grief and groan, to a golden throne, beside the
    King of Heaven."

TO HELEN.

I saw thee once—once only—years ago ;
I must not say how many—but not many.
It was a July midnight ; and from out
A full-orbed moon, that, like thine own soul, soaring,
Sought a precipitate pathway up through heaven,
There fell a silvery-silken veil of light,
With quietude, and sultriness, and slumber,
Upon the upturn'd faces of a thousand
Roses that grew in an enchanted garden,
Where no winds dared to stir, unless on tiptoe—
Fell on the upturned faces of those roses
That gave out, in return for the love-light,
Their odorous souls in an ecstatic death—
Fell on the upturned faces of those roses
That smiled and died in this parterre, enchanted

By thee and by the poetry of thy presence.
Clad all in white, upon a violet bank
I saw thee half reclining ; while the moon
Fell on the upturned faces of the roses,
And on thine own, upturned—alas, in sorrow !

Was it not Fate, that, on this July midnight—
Was it not Fate (whose name is also Sorrow),
That bade me pause before that garden-gate,
To breathe the incense of those slumbering roses ?
No foot-step stirred : the hated world all slept,
Save only thee and me. (Oh, Heaven !—oh, God !
How my heart beats in coupling those two words !)
Save only thee and me. I paused—I looked—
And in an instant all things disappeared.
(Ah, bear in mind this garden was enchanted !)
The pearly lustre of the moon went out :
The mossy banks and the meandering paths,
The happy flowers and repining trees,
Were seen no more ; the very roses' odors
Died in the arms of the adoring airs.
All—all expired save thee—save less than thou:
Save only the divine light in thine eyes—
Save but the soul in thine uplifted eyes.
I saw but them—they were the world to me.
I saw but them—saw only them for hours—
Saw only them until the moon went down.
What wild heart-histories seemed to lie enwritten
Upon those crystalline, celestial spheres !
How dark a woe ! yet how sublime a hope !
How silently serene a sea of pride !
How daring an ambition ! yet how deep—
How fathomless a capacity for love !

But now, at length, dear Dian sank from sight,
Into a western couch of thunder-cloud ;
And thou, a ghost, amid the entombing trees
Didst glide away.   *Only thine eyes remained.*
They *would not* go—they never yet have gone.
Lighting my lonely pathway home that night,
They have not left me (as my hopes have) since.
They follow me—they lead me through the years—
They are my ministers—yet I their slave.
Their office is to illumine and enkindle—
My duty, *to be saved* by their bright light,
And purified by their electric fire,
And sanctified in their elysian fire.
They fill my soul with Beauty (which is Hope),
And are far up in Heaven—the stars I kneel to
In the sad, silent watches of my night ;
While even in the meridian glare of day
I see them still—two sweetly scintillant
Venuses, unextinguished by the sun !

JONES VERY.

It would be a mistake, it is believed, to class Very, as some may have classed him, among minor or obscure poets; for it would be to neglect alike the quality of his inspiration and the tone of his diction. Yet to make this affirmation alone would not be sufficient. We have much reason to think that in greatness as well as in completeness of sincerity, the poems of Very may be taken as those of one of the chief American poets.

Very's outward life, while honorable, was uneventful. Jones Very was born at Salem, Massachusetts, August 28, 1813. In his boyhood he accompanied his father, a shipmaster, on voyages to New Orleans and to Cronstadt. Having entered Harvard in 1834, he was graduated in 1836, and was appointed tutor in Greek, where he was highly esteemed as a teacher. Meantime he studied in the Divinity School. His best literary work was produced at this time. Afterwards, in 1838, he retired to Salem. A volume containing poems and three essays from him appeared in 1839. Throughout his life among those who knew and understood him he commanded the highest respect. After quiet days he died May 8, 1880.

Very has received a rarer and nobler recognition than popularity ; men of genius have concurred in praising him. In respect to his poems and the voice that speaks in them, Bryant, Emerson, and Hawthorne have each paid positive tribute.

The mind from which Very's poetry came was of an unusual order, and one that cannot be judged without special study, though the poetry of that mind may be enjoyed. He was one of those few Americans (perhaps the only American) for whom religious contemplation is everything ; and one of those mortals to whom above others is, in spiritual things, granted the clearest vision. Such a man, as we know with regard to oriental mystics, with whom conditions are more favorable for solitary, rapt meditation than in America, naturally and rightly regards himself as a teacher of divine truth, and an exposer of worldly pretension and sin ; in America less naturally but not less rightly, this was the case with Very.

Very's religion, however, was at its best and strongest in his poems. There his mysticism takes a wide range. With reverence toward God is mingled a joy in the presence of nature, a love of beauty, and a deep perception and firm reproval of sin.

Thus there is something in Very which makes him different from the other American poets. Not that his gift is inferior to theirs ; on the contrary, a perfect vision of eternal things is the truest and most excellent poetry that can exist. It is only necessary to compare Very with the others to perceive that he has also a distinct individuality on the side of character. He has, for example, greater reverence than Emerson; and a purpose more single than Long-fellow's.

Very's thought is not usually difficult of apprehension for any one in the proper mood [1]; though he is never superficial, and his exact meaning cannot be always seen without close attention and without reflection. He may be called an eternal poet in the sense that he treats of the divine state to which mankind will always aspire rather than they will outgrow.

Special reference: *Very's Poems,* edited by James Freeman Clarke. Houghton, Mifflin, & Co.

THE SILENT.

There is a sighing in the wood,
   A murmur in the beating wave,
The heart has never understood
   To tell in words the thoughts they gave.

Yet oft it feels an answering tone,
   When wandering on the lonely shore;
And could the lips its voice make known,
   'T would sound as does the ocean's roar.

And oft beneath the wind-swept pine
   Some chord is struck the strain to swell;
Nor sounds nor language can define,—
   'T is not for words or sounds to tell.

[1] The reader should instead doubt his own fitness.

'T is all unheard, that Silent Voice,
  Whose goings forth, unknown to all,
Bids bending reed and bird rejoice,
  And fills with music Nature's hall.

And in the speechless human heart
  It speaks where'er man's feet have trod,
Beyond the lips' deceitful art,
  To tell of Him, the Unseen God.

THE RIVER.

Oh ! swell my bosom deeper with thy love,
  That I some river's widening mouth may be ;
And ever on, for many a mile above,
  May flow the floods that enter from thy sea ;
And may they not retreat as tides of earth,
  Save but to flow from Thee that they have flown,
Soon may my spirit find that better birth,
  Where the retiring wave is never known ;
But Thou dost flow through every channel wide,
  With all a Father's love in every soul ;
A stream that knows no ebb, a swelling tide
  That rolls forever on and finds no goal,
Till in the hearts of all shall opened be
The ocean depths of thine eternity.

YOURSELF.

'T is to yourself I speak ; you cannot know
  Him whom I call in speaking such a one,
For you beneath the earth lie buried low,
  Which he alone as living walks upon :

You may at times have heard him speak to you,
  And often wished perchance that you were he ;
And I must ever wish that it were true,
  For then you could hold fellowship with me ;
But now you hear us talk as strangers, met
  Above the room wherein you lie abed ;
A word perhaps loud spoken you may get,
  Or hear our feet when heavily they tread ;
But he who speaks, or him who 's spoken to,
Must both remain as strangers still to you.

NATURE.

Nature ! my love for thee is deeper far
  Than strength of words, though spirit-born, can tell :
For while I gaze they seem my soul to bar,
  That in thy widening streams would onward swell,
Bearing thy mirrored beauty on its breast,—
  Now through thy lonely haunts unseen to glide,
A motion that scarce knows itself from rest,
  With pictured flowers and branches on its tide ;
Then by the noisy city's frowning wall,
  Whose armed heights within its waters gleam,
To rush with answering voice to ocean's call,
  And mingle with the deep its swollen stream,
Whose boundless bosom's calm alone can hold
That heaven of glory in thy skies unrolled.

THE TREES OF LIFE.

For those who worship Thee there is no death,
  For all they do is but with Thee to dwell :
Now while I take from Thee this passing breath,
  It is but of thy glorious name to tell ;

Nor words nor measured sounds have I to find,
  But in them both my soul doth ever flow ;
They come as viewless as the unseen wind,
  And tell thy noiseless steps where'er I go ;
The trees that grow along thy living stream,
  And from its springs refreshment ever drink,
Forever glittering in thy morning beam
  They bend them o'er the river's grassy brink,
And, as more high and wide their branches grow,
They look more fair within the depths below.

HENRY WADSWORTH LONGFELLOW.

Longfellow has added the sense of fancy to American life. As a poet he is distinguished in American literature for imagination in his literary treatment and for largeness and skill in the framing of his ideas and pictures. At the time he wrote he cast his seed into a warm, moist soil already fertilized by previous literary efforts. As a man his life is full of charm and of suggestiveness for study.[1]

Henry Wadsworth Longfellow was born at Portland, Maine, February 22, 1807. His father was a man much honored in the state; it was from his mother that he inherited a taste for romance.[2] In his home he had access to Shakespeare, Milton, Thomson, Goldsmith, Johnson's *Lives of the Poets*, Plutarch's *Lives* and the like. "As a boy he was of a tender, sensitive disposition," but was also "the sunlight of the house."[3]

[1] His biography by his brother, Rev. Samuel Longfellow, has merit not only for authenticity, but for the fulness with which we see the personality and the humanity of the most lovable of American characters.

[2] While he was in college he corresponded with his mother on the subject of Gray's Odes, for instance, expressing his admiration of them. In reply she stated her own poetical opinions and observations.—*Life*, vol. i., pp. 29–32.

[3] For a glimpse of his home in childhood, see *ibid*, vol. i., pp. 14, 15.

In 1821 he entered Bowdoin, where, in his observ-
ance of regular study and in his pursuit of general
literature, he seems to have been one of those who
have the strength and poise for success both in duty
and in ambition.

Graduating in 1825, he spent from 1826 to 1829
travelling and studying in continental Europe ; was
professor of modern languages at Bowdoin from
1829 to 1835 ; and after another year abroad, occu-
pied the same position at Harvard from 1835 till
1856.

Longfellow's earlier poems, which were written before he was nineteen, show the influence of Bryant,
but no sign of his own later power, his rich nature
requiring the favor of many literary conditions and
of much stimulus before it would fully come forth ;
for a dozen years he wrote not a single original poem.

In 1833 Longfellow published his stately translation of the *Coplas* of Manrique, who was one of a
number of modern poets Longfellow handled in a
similar way.   In 1835 he put forth *Outre Mer*, a suc-
cession of papers having a general resemblance to
Irving's *Sketch-Book*,[1] but by the thread of their
narrative connected more closely together.

Four years later appeared *Hyperion*, a second
prose romance, which was strongly suggestive of the
interest in German literature then becoming active.
From this source, and from his study of the Greek
poets, is partly due the inspiration of Longfellow's
poems *Flowers, A Psalm of Life,* and others in the

---

[1] Longfellow, while writing the *Hyperion* had this resemblance in
mind.   The *Sketch-Book* was also Longfellow's first favorite volume.

Voices of the Night, which was published, like *Hyperion*, in 1839.

Longfellow's first truly poetical inspiration did not find him unprepared. His early modest sense of immaturity and littleness before the great works upon which he had for several years been musing, had led him to sympathetic study. Now, in 1839, he had his materials ready and his sensibilities trained. If he wanted anything from foreign literature to aid him in the composition of a poem, he knew readily where he could find what he desired. He had also acquired taste, appreciation, a sense of proportion, a true perception of the beautiful, and unusual technical skill. Accordingly, from the *Voices of the Night* on, his works flowed from him easily and increased rapidly in strength and variety, for he had then merely to perform that difficult literary function which deals with the concrete expression of the beautiful, or in its higher form with the harmonious creating and proportioning which constitutes imagination.

The *Skeleton in Armor*, the outcome of about two years' brooding and painstaking, was a long step forward. Still more reproductive of the old ballad is the *Wreck of the Hesperus*. About the same time came the popular *Village Blacksmith*. Among others of about the same date, *The Slave Singing at Midnight* has an unconscious power of outspokenness; *The Spanish Student*, a play, is the most ambitious of Longfellow's writings up to this time[1];

---

[1] Note, however, the pleasing and graceful scene between Vittorio and Preciosa.

and *The Arsenal at Springfield, The Bridge,* and *The Old Clock on the Stairs* are, each in their own way, of conspicuous merit.

In 1847, with *Evangeline,* Longfellow's first successful poem which was written in hexameter verse, he sounded a deeper and more sustained pathos than ever before. *Kavanagh,* in 1849, a prose tale, containing an occasional note of gentle satire,[1] is a series of pleasant pictures of New England life and sentiment half a century ago. Shorter poems with subjects well treated are *The Building of the Ship, The Light-House,* and *The Fire of Drift-Wood.*

In 1851, Longfellow published *The Golden Legend,* the first of the trilogy, the *Christus,* on which he labored from the time of its first conception for over thirty years.[2] *The Golden Legend* on a sacred theme continues the strain of pathos shown by Longfellow in *Evangeline,* and deals with the spirit of Christianity as revealed in the Middle Ages.

The Song of Hiawatha, in 1855, has been called America's first contribution to world literature. In this poem, Longfellow, having perceived the poetic capabilities of the Indian legends, welded them into a whole, the life of which is quickened by invention of his own. A breath of nature passes over the pages, and the public attention hitherto paid to the mechanism and commonplace narratives

---

[1] Such as the exquisite Chapter XX., with its caricature in the personage, Hathaway, and with the suggestive truth of its discussion.

[2] 1841–1873.

5

of the poem may well be turned to the higher flights of fancy and imagination.[1]

In 1846, Longfellow, while visiting Portland, meditated a poem on his old home, and nine years later wrote *My Lost Youth*. A little later came *The Children's Hour*, *Paul Revere's Ride*, and the fine lyric, *The Bells of Lynn*.

The Courtship of Miles Standish, in 1858, is a well-told and very life-like story in hexameters. An excellent, serious shorter poem of about the same time is the *Warden of the Cinque Ports*.

Longfellow's translation of the *Divine Comedy*, which appeared several years later, is the best English version. Not only is the original rendered line for line, but the translation itself has a poetic charm thrown around it.

The New England Tragedies, in 1869, made up the second part issued of Longfellow's sacred trilogy. The first of these two pathetic plays images the persecution of the Quakers by Endicott, who was himself in the power of the harsh superstition which was part of his creed. In the second tragedy, it is the fear of witchcraft which moves men to sacrifice their victims. Two years later, the third part of the trilogy, *The Divine Tragedy*, narrated in verse the story of the gospels, drawing from these the words of Christus, but imagining those of the minor personages. Among Longfellow's best subsequent poems are *The Four Lakes of Madison* and *The Leap of Roushan Beg*. *Michael Angelo*, a long poem,

---

[1] To the beautiful description, for example, of the combat between Hiawatha and Mudjekeewis.

has a spirituality as noble and impassioned as any poem in American literature. Longfellow died March 24, 1882.

Longfellow's greatest works, *Evangeline, Hiawatha,* and *The New England Tragedies,* and among shorter poems *The Skeleton in Armor* and *The Wreck of the Hesperus,* are on American subjects. Yet his greatness over the other poets of this country is that he has interested, not this nation alone, but mankind.

Special references: Longfellow's Poetical Works ; Longfellow's Life, edited by Rev. S. Longfellow. Houghton, Mifflin, & Co.

THE SKELETON IN ARMOR.[1]

"Speak ! speak ! thou fearful guest !
Who, with thy hollow breast
Still in rude armor drest,
   Comest to daunt me !
Wrapt not in Eastern balms,
But with thy fleshless palms
Stretched, as if asking alms,
   Why dost thou haunt me ? "

Then, from those cavernous eyes
Pale flashes seemed to rise,
As when the Northern skies
   Gleam in December ;
And, like the water's flow
Under December's snow,

[1] *The Skeleton in Armor*, found at the ruins of the round tower at Newport, R. I.

Came a dull voice of woe
   From the heart's chamber.

" I was a viking old !
My deeds though manifold,
No Skald [1] in song has told,
   No Saga [2] taught thee !
Take heed, that in thy verse
Thou dost the tale rehearse,
Else dread a dead man's curse ;
   For this I sought thee.

" Far in the Northern land,
By the wild Baltic's strand,
I, with my childish hand,
   Tamed the gerfalcon ;
And, with my skates fast-bound,
Skimmed the half-frozen Sound,
That the poor whimpering hound
   Trembled to walk on.

" Oft to his frozen lair
Tracked I the grisly bear,
While from my path the hare
   Fled like a shadow ;
Oft through the forest dark
Followed the were-wolf's bark,
Until the soaring lark
Sang from the meadow.

" But when I older grew,
   Joining a corsair's [3] crew,

---

[1] *Skald*, an ancient Scandinavian bard.
[2] *Saga*, an ancient heroic Scandinavian tale.   [3] *Corsair*, a pirate.

O'er the dark sea I flew
  With the marauders.
Wild was the life we led ;
Many the souls that sped,
Many the hearts that bled,
  By our stern orders.

" Many a wassail-bout [1]
Wore the long Winter out ;
Often our midnight shout
  Set the cocks crowing,
As we the Berserk's tale
Measured in cups of ale,
Draining the oaken pail,
  Filled to o'erflowing.

" Once as I told in glee
Tales of the stormy sea,
Soft eyes did gaze on me,
  Burning yet tender ;
And as the white stars shine
On the dark Norway pine,
On that dark heart of mine
  Fell their soft splendor.

" I wooed the blue-eyed maid,
Yielding, yet half afraid,
And in the forest's shade,
  Our vows were plighted.
Under its loosened vest
Fluttered her little breast,
Like birds within their nest,
  By the hawk frighted.

---

[1] *Wassail-bout*, a drinking bout.

" Bright in her father's hall
Shields gleamed upon the wall,
Loud sang the minstrels all,
    Chanting his glory ;
When of old Hildebrand
I asked his daughter's hand,
Mute did the minstrels stand
    To hear my story.

" While the brown ale he quaffed,
Loud then the champion laughed,
And as the wind-gusts waft
    The sea-foam brightly,
So the loud laugh of scorn,
Out of those lips unshorn,
From the deep drinking-horn
    Blew the foam lightly.

"She was a prince's child,
I but a Viking wild,
And though she blushed and smiled,
    I was discarded !
Should not the dove so white
Follow the sea-mew's flight,
Why did they leave that night
    Her nest unguarded ?

" Scarce had I put to sea,
Bearing the maid with me,
Fairest of all was she
    Among the Norsemen !
When on the white sea-strand,
Waving his armèd hand,

Saw we old Hildebrand,
  With twenty horsemen.

" Then launched they to the blast,
Bent like a reed each mast,
Yet we were gaining fast,
  When the wind failed us ;
And with a sudden flaw
Came round the gusty Skaw,[1]
So that our foe we saw
  Laugh as he hailed us.

" And as to catch the gale
Round veered the flapping sail,
Death ! was the helmsman's hail,
  Death without quarter !
Mid-ships with iron keel
Struck we her ribs of steel ;
Down her black hulk did reel ;
  Through the black water !

" As with his wings aslant,
Sails the fierce cormorant,
Seeking some rocky haunt,
  With his prey laden,
So toward the open main,
Beating to sea again,
Through the wild hurricane,
  Bore I the maiden.

" Three weeks we westward bore,
And when the storm was o'er,

---

[1] *Skaw*, a promontory.

Cloud-like we saw the shore
   Stretching to leeward ;
There for my lady's bower
Built I the lofty tower,
Which to this very hour.
   Stands looking seaward.

" There lived we many years ;
Time dried the maiden's tears ;
She had forgot her fears,
   She was a mother ;
Death closed her mild blue eyes,
Under that tower she lies ;
Ne'er shall the sun arise
   On such another.

" Still grew my bosom then,
Still as a stagnant fen !
Hateful to me were men,
   The sunlight hateful !
In the vast forest here,
Clad in my warlike gear,
Fell I upon my spear,
   O, death was grateful !

" Thus, seamed with many scars,
Bursting these prison bars,
Up to its native stars
   My soul ascended !
There from the flowing bowl
Deep drinks the warrior's soul,
Skoal ! to the Northland ! *skoal !* "
   Thus the tale ended.

[1] *Skoal,* "an exclamation of good wishes."

MY LOST YOUTH.

Often I think of the beautiful town [1]
  That is seated by the sea ;
Often in thought go up and down
The pleasant streets of that dear old town,
  And my youth comes back to me.
    And a verse of a Lapland song
    Is haunting my memory still,
    "A boy's will is the wind's will,
And the thoughts of youth are long, long thoughts."

I can see the shadowy lines of its trees,
  And catch, in sudden gleams,
The sheen of the far-surrounding seas,
And islands that were the Hesperides [2]
  Of all my boyish dreams.
    And the burden of that old song,
    It murmurs and whispers still :
    "A boy's will is the wind's will,
And the thoughts of youth are long, long thoughts."

I remember the black wharves and the slips,
  And the sea-tides tossing free ;
And Spanish sailors [3] with bearded lips,
And the beauty and mystery of the ships,
  And the magic of the sea.
    And the voice of that wayward song
    Is singing and saying still :

[1] *Town*, Portland, Maine.

[2] *Hesperides*, islands and gardens referred to by the ancients, and ocated to the west of them. *See Anthon's Class. Dict., Hesperides md Hesperidum Insulæ.*

[3] *Spanish sailors*, engaged in the trade from the West Indies.

" A boy's will is the wind's will,
And the thoughts of youth are long, long thoughts."

I remember the bulwarks by the shore,
    And the fort upon the hill ;
The sunrise gun, with its hollow roar
The drum-beat repeated o'er and o'er,
    And the bugle wild and shrill.
        And the music of that old song
        Throbs in my memory still :
    " A boy's will is the wind's will,
And the thoughts of youth are long, long thoughts."

I remember the sea-fight far away,
    How it thundered o'er the tide !
And the dead captains as they lay
In their graves, o'erlooking the tranquil bay,
    Where they in battle died.
        And the sound of that mournful song
        Goes through me with a thrill :
    " A boy's will is the wind's will,
And the thoughts of youth are long, long thoughts."

I can see the breezy dome of groves,
    The shadows of Deering's woods ;
And the friendships old, and the early loves
Come back with a sabbath sound, as of doves
    In quiet neighborhoods.
        And the verse of that sweet old song,
        It flutters and murmurs still :
    " A boy's will is the wind's will,
And the thoughts of youth are long, long thoughts."

I remember the gleams and glooms that dart
  Across the school-boy's brain ;
The song and the silence in the heart,
That in part are prophecies, and in part
  Are longings wild and vain.
    And the voice of that fitful song
    Sings on, and is never still :
    " A boy's will is the wind's will,
And the thoughts of youth are long, long
      thoughts."

There are things of which I may not speak ;
  There are dreams that cannot die ;
There are thoughts that make the strong
      heart weak,
And bring a pallor into the cheek,
  And a mist before the eye.
    And the words of that fatal song
    Come over me like a chill :
    " A boy's will is the wind's will,
And the thoughts of youth are long, long
      thoughts."

Strange to me now are the forms I meet
  When I visit the dear old town ;
But the native air is pure and sweet,
And the trees that o'ershadow each well-
      known street,
  As they balance up and down,
    Are singing the beautiful song,
    Are sighing and whispering still :
    " A boy's will is the wind's will,
And the thoughts of youth are long, long
      thoughts."

And Deering's Woods are fresh and fair,
  And with joy that is almost pain
My heart goes back to wander there,
And among the dreams of days that were,
  I find my lost youth again.
    And the strange and beautiful song,
    The groves are repeating it still:
  "A boy's will is the wind's will,
And the thoughts of youth are long, long
      thoughts."

DANTE.

Tuscan,[1] that wanderest through the realms of gloom,
  With thoughtful pace, and sad, majestic eyes,
  Stern thoughts and awful from thy soul arise,
Like Farinata[2] from his fiery tomb.
Thy sacred song is like the trump of doom;
  Yet in thy heart what human sympathies,
  What soft compassion glows, as in the skies
The tender stars their clouded lamps relume!
Methinks I see thee stand, with pallid cheeks,
  By Fra Hilario[3] in his diocese,
As up the convent-walls, in golden streaks,
  The ascending sunbeams mark the day's decrease;
And, as he asks what there the stranger seeks,
  Thy voice along the cloister whispers, "Peace!"

[1] *Tuscan*, Florence, Dante's birthplace, is in Tuscany.
[2] *Farinata*, a nobleman of Florence placed by Dante in his *Inferno* in a red-hot coffin.
[3] *Fra Hilario.* See Leigh Hunt's account of Dante's errand.

JAMES RUSSELL LOWELL.

Like Longfellow, Lowell represents not alone the country which was his birth-place and the life of which he reflects; he also embodies a continuation of the spirit of the literature whose tongue he spoke, though his best topics touch American soil, or appeal to American hearts, as in the *Biglow Papers* and the Harvard *Commemoration Ode*.

James Russell Lowell was born in Cambridge, Massachusetts, February 22, 1819. From his ancestry his mental inheritance comprised both intellectual strength and the light grace of fancy. His grandfather, Judge John Lowell, won public respect and confidence; his father, Rev. Dr. Charles Lowell, studied in the universities of two worlds[1] and was the writer of several works; and his mother brought Lowell up in her own love of language and of the old ballads.[2] Furthermore, at Lowell's home there was a large and choice library of modern masterpieces, which he not only read extensively, but, what is rarer, knew how to assimilate the parts that concerned himself.

[1] Harvard and Edinburgh. Study abroad was not common then.
[2] It is said that she sang them over the cradles of her children.

Lowell was graduated at Harvard in 1838. Three years later he published his first volume of poems, *A Year's Life*, and in 1844 a second volume. All the pieces from these two volumes which their author preserved have their respective merit: such poems as Lowell's love songs, his descriptions of nature, and his *Ode*, in which a mightier purpose emerges, and which in better and stronger fulfilment is found later transfigured in the *Commemoration Ode*. *Freedom* is the sincerest poem, at least before the *Biglow Papers*, that he ever wrote. In all his early production, the aim is serious, the conceptions powerful, and the accomplishment marked by grace and vigor. Yet in none of them had beauty reached through him its full expression, nor had moral indignation, though in evidence, yet found its most effective utterance.

Before Lowell was thirty years of age, he had written the *Vision of Sir Launfal*, the *Fable for Critics*, and the first series of the *Biglow Papers*,— productions in which he proved himself to be a poet of great power and of abundant resources of style and imagery. In *Sir Launfal*, for the first time with Lowell, the tone of Christian morality is equalled by the beauty of varied materials; and the observation of nature and the contemplation of human life become broader and more poetic. The *Fable for Critics*, although open to the charge of hastiness in some of its judgments, is a frank and strong poem. It should be observed that qualities in it which might seem defects now were the opposite then; as may be illustrated in Lowell's early discernment there of the high station of Whittier and of Hawthorne, the former of whom had not yet reached perfection in verse, nor had the latter then written a great romance.

The *Biglow Papers*, the first proof of Lowell's genius as a national poet, is of most importance as expressing the best elements of the national character up to that time; and of subordinate value as a satire of follies of the day and as a vehicle for exhibiting the Yankee dialect and manners. The seriousness of the motive of the work should carefully be discerned, the exuberant wit and humor in the *Biglow Papers* existing only to insure that the arrow of deep indignation should come to its mark on the light feather of grace and dialect.

From the time of publication of the first series of the *Biglow Papers*, for nearly twenty years, Lowell published no important verse, with the exception of the *Biglow Papers, Second Series*, which differed from the first principally in being more serious in style. During the interval Lowell was at first abroad, then succeeded to Longfellow's chair at Harvard, and afterwards became editor successively of the *Atlantic Monthly* and of the *North American Review*. In 1864, he published *Fireside Travels*.

The *Commemoration Ode*, a year later, was a revelation even to Lowell himself of a power in him far higher than any he had exercised hitherto, or exercised afterwards to the same perfection. The *Ode* contains passages that for true sublimity are transcended by those of no ode in the English language. In timeliness of utterance Lowell's ode surpasses all others. In the author, its echoes ring still loud and clear in Lowell's *Concord Ode*, or in the ode *Under the Old Elm*, where Washington draws his sword with such consequences.

After the production of *Under the Willows*, containing the modest *Agro Dolce* and the charming *Auf Wiedersehen*, the *Cathedral* rises forth at Lowell's farthest reach of reflection. Large, profoundest meditation on a great theme is the kernel; and such vision of the deep things perceived in nature and humanity is, when leading to the spiritual vision of the workings of God, the essence of the highest poetry.

In 1870, Lowell published two volumes of essays, written in an attractive style, *My Study Windows* and *Among my Books, First Series*. In order to read them with appreciation, however, as well as enjoyment, it is necessary for the reader to have, to start with, a fair amount of scholarship himself; he will then find that his admiration of them grows with the increase in his own knowledge and sincerity. *Among my Books, Second Series*, is, if possible, still more scholarly. In the main the three volumes exhibit genius interpreting genius less familiar to the American who peruses them. Less elaborate in style and in matter, but hardly less valuable are the remaining prose works of Lowell, *Democracy and Other Essays, Political Essays*,[1] *Latest Literary Essays*, and the *Old English Dramatists*.

In *Heartsease and Rue*, written at the sunset of Lowell's life, his genius casts its light about more

---

[1] Especially the essay last in order.

softly beautiful than ever before. *Heartsease and Rue, Agassiz, Tempora Mutantur*, and *Fitz-Adams' Story*, with the well-drawn sketch of the gentle cynic who is the principal character, are longer poems of various notes. In the shorter ones of sentiment the wonderful youthfulness of the author seems to have been waiting its expression because he had all his life wished to take weightier things first. Lowell died August 12, 1891.

First and foremost, Lowell is the American poet of patriotism. In his song for his country, the essential ideas, while against national selfishness, vanity, or aggrandizement, also inspire the reader toward justice and freedom; and he has scourged base politicians as he would have done in any country so fortunate as to have been his birthplace.

As a critic, Lowell was more than brilliant or witty; qualities of this sort were in him subordinate to ethical aims and standards. The latter dominated a literary purpose which makes his essays interesting to those who enjoy letters not for mere drudgery nor for dilettanteism; for in literature, as well as in life, the minor graces and virtues were held by him in subordination. He made sure of the main things, and took so much of the rest as came along with them.

For the moral element is the central one in Lowell—the one around which all the others crystallize. In support of that, satire was a weapon; for the sake of that, love shows its most beautiful aspects; to strengthen that, scholarship is turned on the most healthful subjects; to secure that, poetry glorifies

6

public virtue. Even strong love for genius is repressed, when its utterance might appear to extol
weak character.

Together with this moral element, and springing
from it, goes, closely connected, Lowell's insight,
which made him not only a writer of powerful verse,
and an appreciative student of the genius of the best
poets, but also a critic of political life, and a man of
felicity and high success as a foreign minister.

With some American authors, especially with Poe,
one perusal gives all that the general reader can
profit by; but Lowell, even when familiar, is an
author still to be read; and in the extension alike of
scholarship and of national integrity, his power will
yet be useful. For the future, his literary essays
have surely fruit to bear—perhaps most of their
fruit—in the labor of others: for, with the study of
the best modern literature, will go on in this country
the examination of his literary observations. His
poetry is largely unassimilated by the mass of American readers, and calls for greater depth and intensity
of study than have ever been given.

Special references: Lowell's Poetical Works and *Heartsease and
Rue.* Houghton, Mifflin & Co. Norton's *Letters of Lowell.* Har-
pers. Underwood's *The Poet and the Man.* Houghton, Mifflin
& Co.

ODE.

I.

In the old days of awe and keen-eyed wonder,[1]
The Poet's song with blood-warm truth was rife;

[1] *Cf.* Puttenham's *Art of English Poesie.*

He saw the mysteries which circle under
    The outward shell and skin of daily life.
Nothing to him were fleeting time and fashion,
    His soul was led by the eternal law ;
There was in him no hope of fame, no passion,
    But with calm, godlike eyes he only saw.
He did not sigh o'er heroes dead and buried,
    Chief-mourner at the Golden Age's hearse,
Nor deem that souls whom Charon[1] grim had ferried
    Alone were fitting themes of epic verse :
He could believe the promise of to-morrow,
    And feel the wondrous meaning of to-day ;
He had a deeper faith in holy sorrow
    Than the world's seeming loss could take away.
To know the heart of all things was his duty,
    All things did sing to him to make him wise,
And with a sorrowful and conquering beauty,
    The soul of all looked grandly from his eyes.
He gazed on all within him and without him,
    He watched the flowing of Time's steady tide,
And shapes of glory floated all about him
    And whispered to him, and he prophesied.
Than all men he more fearless was and freer,
    And all his brethren cried with one accord,—
" Behold the holy man ! Behold the Seer !
    Him who hath spoken with the unseen Lord ! "
He to his heart with large embrace had taken
    The universal sorrow of mankind,
And, from that root, a shelter never shaken,
    The tree of wisdom grew with sturdy rind.
He could interpret well the wondrous voices
    Which to the calm and silent spirit come ;

---

[1] *Charon*, the ferryman in classic legend to the infernal regions.

He knew that the One Soul no more rejoices
   In the star's anthem than the insect's hum.
He in his heart was ever meek and humble,
   And yet with kingly pomp his numbers ran,
As he foresaw how all things false should crumble
   Before the free, uplifted soul of man :
And, when he was made full to overflowing
   With all the loveliness of heaven and earth,
Out rushed his song, like molten iron glowing,
   To show God sitting by the humblest hearth.
With calmest courage he was ever ready
   To teach that action was the truth of thought,
And, with strong arm and purpose firm and steady,
   An anchor for the drifting world he wrought.
So did he make the meanest man partaker
   Of all his brother-gods unto him gave ;
All souls did reverence him and name him Maker,
   And when he died heaped temples on his grave.
And still his deathless words of light are swimming
   Serene throughout the great deep infinite
Of human soul, unwaning, and undimming,
   To cheer and guide the mariner at night.

II.

But now the Poet is an empty rhymer
   Who lies with idle elbow on the grass,
And fits his singing, like a cunning timer,
   To all men's prides and fancies as they pass.
Not his the song, which, in its metre holy,
   Chimes with the music of the eternal stars,
Humbling the tyrant, lifting up the lowly,
   And sending sun through the soul's prison-bars.

Maker no more,—O no! unmaker rather,
  For he unmakes who doth not all put forth
The power given freely by our loving Father
  To show the body's dross, the spirit's worth.
Awake! great spirit of the ages olden!
  Shiver the mists that hide thy starry lyre,
And let man's soul be yet again beholden
  To thee for wings to soar to her desire.
O, prophesy no more to-morrow's splendor,
  Be no more shamefaced to speak out for Truth,
Lay on her altar all the gushings tender,
  The hope, the fire, the loving faith of youth!
O, prophesy no more the Maker's coming,
  Say not his onward footsteps thou canst hear
In the dim void, like to the awful humming
  Of the great wings of some new-lighted sphere!
O, prophesy no more, but be the Poet!
  This longing was but granted unto thee
That, when all beauty thou should'st feel and know it,
  That beauty in its highest thou couldst be.
O thou who moanest tost with sealike longings,
  Who dimly hearest voices call on thee,
Whose soul is overfilled with mighty throngings
  Of love, and fear, and glorious agony,
Thou of the toil-strung hands and iron sinews
  And soul by Mother Earth with freedom fed,
In whom the hero-spirit yet continues,
  The old free nature is not chained or dead,
Arouse! let thy soul break in music-thunder,
  Let loose the ocean that is in thee pent,
Pour forth thy hope, thy fear, thy love, thy wonder,
  And tell the age what all its signs have meant.
Where'er thy wildered crowd of brethren jostles,

Where'er there lingers but a shadow of wrong,
There still is need of martyrs and apostles,
    There still are texts for never-dying song :
From age to age man's still aspiring spirit
    Finds wider scope and sees with clearer eyes,
And thou in larger measure dost inherit
    What made thy great forerunners free and wise.
Sit thou enthroned where the Poet's mountain
    Above the thunder lifts its silent peak,
And roll thy songs down like a gathering fountain,
    They all may drink and find the rest they seek.
Sing ! there shall silence grow in earth and heaven,
    A silence of deep awe and wondering ;
For, listening gladly, bend the angels even,
    To hear a mortal like an angel sing.

III.

Among the toil-worn poor my soul is seeking
    For who shall bring the Maker's name to light,
To be the voice of that almighty speaking
    Which every age demands to do it right.
Proprieties our silken bards environ ;
    He who would be the tongue of this wide land
Must string his harp with chords of sturdy iron
    And strike it with a toil imbrowned hand :
One who hath dwelt with Nature well attended,
    Who hath learnt wisdom from her mystic books,
Whose soul with all her countless lives hath blended,
    So that all beauty awes us in his looks ;
Who not with body's waste his soul hath pampered,
    Who as the clear northwestern wind is free,
Who walks with Form's observances unhampered,
    And follows the One Will obediently ;

Whose eyes, like windows on a breezy summit,
  Control a lovely prospect every way ;
Who doth not sound God's sea with earthly plummet,
  And find a bottom still of worthless clay ;
Who heeds not how the lower gusts are working,
  Knowing that one sure wind blows on above,
And sees, beneath the foulest faces lurking,
  One God-built shrine of reverence and love ;
Who sees all stars that wheel their shining marches
  Around the centre fixed of Destiny,
Where the encircling soul serene o'erarches
  The moving globe of being like a sky ;
Who feels that God and Heaven's great deeps are nearer
  Him to whose heart his fellow-man is nigh,
Who doth not hold his soul's own freedom dearer
  Than that of all his brethren, low or high ;
Who to the Right can feel himself the truer
  For being gently patient with the wrong,
Who sees a brother in the evil-doer,
  And finds in Love the heart's-blood of his song ;—
This, this is he for whom the world is waiting,
  To sing the beatings of its mighty heart,
Too long hath it been patient with the grating
  Of scrannel-pipes, [1] and heard it misnamed Art.
To him the smiling soul of man shall listen,
  Laying awhile its crown of thorns aside,
And once again in every eye shall glisten
  The glory of a nature satisfied.
His verse shall have a great commanding motion,
  Heaving and swelling with a melody
Learnt of the sky, the river, and the ocean,
  And all the pure, majestic things that be.

---

[1] *Scrannel*, miserable ; a word not now in prose usage.

Awake, then, thou ! we pine for thy great presence
  To make us feel the soul once more sublime,
We are of far too infinite an essence
  To rest contented with the lies of Time.
Speak out ! and lo ! a hush of deepest wonder
  Shall sink o'er all this many-voiced scene,
As when a sudden burst of rattling thunder
  Shatters the blueness of a sky serene.

TO CHARLES ELIOT NORTON. [1]

AGRO-DOLCE. [2]

The wind is roistering out of doors,
My windows shake and my chimney roars ;
My Elmwood[3] chimneys seem crooning to me,
As of old, in their moody, minor key,
And out of the past the hoarse wind blows,
As I sit in my arm-chair, and toast my toes.

"Ho ! ho ! nine-and-forty," they seem to sing,
" We saw you a little toddling thing.
We knew you child and youth and man,
A wonderful fellow to dream and plan,
With a great thing always to come,—who knows ?
Well, well ! 't is some comfort to toast one's toes.

" How many times have you sat at gaze
Till the mouldering fire forgot to blaze,

---

[1] *Charles Eliot Norton*, writer on the fine arts and translator of Dante ; born at Cambridge, Mass., in 1829.

[2] *Agro-dolce*, bitter-sweet.

[3] *Elmwood*, the residence of the poet at Cambridge.

Shaping among the whimsical coals
Fancies and figures and shining goals !
What matters the ashes that cover those ?
While hickory lasts you can toast your toes.

"O dream-ship-builder ! where are they all,
Your grand three-deckers, deep-chested and tall,
That should crush the waves under canvas piles,
And anchor at last by the Fortunate Isles ?
There 's gray in your beard, the years turn foes,
While you muse in your arm-chair, and toast your toes."

I sit and dream that I hear, as of yore,
My Elmwood chimneys' deep-throated roar ;
If much be gone, there is much remains ;
By the embers of loss I count my gains,
You and yours with the best, till the old hope glows
In the fanciful flame, as I toast my toes.

Instead of a fleet of broad-browed ships,
To send a child's armada of chips !
Instead of the great guns, tier on tier,
A freight of pebbles and grass-blades sere !
"Well, maybe more love with the less gift goes,"
I growl, as, half moody, I toast my toes.

AUF WIEDERSEHEN ![1]

SUMMER.

The little gate was reached at last,
　Half hid in lilacs down the lane ;
She pushed it wide, and, as she past,

[1] *Auf Wiederschen*, till we meet again.

A wistful look she backward cast,
  And said,—"*Auf Wiedersehen!*"

With hand on latch, a vision white
  Lingered reluctant, and again
Half doubting if she did aright,
Soft as the dews that fell that night,
  She said,—"*Auf Wiedersehen!*"

The lamp's clear gleam flits up the stair ;
  I linger in delicious pain ;
Ah, in that chamber, whose rich air
To breathe in thought I scarcely dare,
  Thinks she,—"*Auf Wiedersehen!*"

'T is thirteen years ; once more I press
  The turf that silences the lane ;
I hear the rustle of her dress,
I smell the lilacs, and—ah, yes,
  I hear "*Auf Wiedersehen!*"

Sweet piece of bashful maiden art !
  The English words had seemed too fain,
But these—they drew us heart to heart,
Yet held us tenderly apart ;
  She said, "*Auf Wiedersehen!*"

OLIVER WENDELL HOLMES.

Verse may have other aims than to convey aspiration; it can serve to correct folly and to point the moral of better manners and better sense. Such an end satisfies towns-people; they like to see their sentiment of good-fellowship broadened and more thoroughly enlivened, as well as any eccentricity among them lopped away by the keen knife of ridicule. A poet who can do these things well, receives popularity, as Holmes does; though Holmes is not this alone, being capable also in poetry of dealing with philosophical truth.

Oliver Wendell Holmes was born at Cambridge, Massachusetts, August 29, 1809. He graduated at Harvard in 1829, and after several years' professional study in Europe, took his degree of Doctor of Medicine in 1836. For a part of his life he has been a professor of medicine, but for a still longer period a man of letters. His work as an author embraces poetry, prose, fiction, and the familiar essay.

The Breakfast Table Series, the best known among his prose writings, is, in certain ways, paralleled in his verse. In both he treats of matters of life which are to many of the community serious and important,—to that part especially whom we hear alluded to as having had the advantages of education, and who feel that they can profit by a rhymed sermon compounded to be at once palatable and electrical, but whose intellectual disinterestedness stops here. For to this part of the educated as well as the uneducated class, the savor of learning is better than the toil of scholarship, and it is a great deal easier; to them, too, science is made to play with, rather than to work out, and a society that chats is far more satisfactory than one that is in earnest.

Dr. Holmes understands all this, no one better. The unimaginative reader would make the mistake of classifying the author as superficial; let him try, then, to vie with the Autocrat! The truth is, that he must be at once a wit, a man of the world, and a gentleman, who can detect the absurd, expose the pretentious, and denounce the vulgar as cleverly and unerringly as Holmes does. The keys to his satire are not so common that they are easily found and made use of.

But Holmes is not a satirist alone. He has an eye for character, and especially for oddity. Witness his *One Hoss Shay, How the Old Horse Won the Bet,* and *On Lending a Punch-Bowl,* in which the humorous qualities of the subject chosen are woven into his work. His feelings overflow in another sense in the social verses *At the Saturday Club, A Farewell to Agassiz,* and *The Semi-Centennial Celebration of the New England Society. The Opening of the Piano* is also distinctive, but its smart point at the close is in a style too much imitated later by writers for children.

The verses on *Dorothy Q.* show the interest with which Holmes can surround what in itself is uninteresting. Another view of women, *La Grisette*, is piquant and sparkling,—one of Holmes's best. The lines dance along as heartily and merrily as the mind of the imaginary beholder, and as musically and harmoniously as rhythm should always run. *Iris, Her Book*, is a poem dealing with a complex and usually uncomprehended nature, and in it Holmes evinces by the pathos he casts about it, to what length his strength and sympathy can go.

The poet's feeling widens to patriotism both for New England and for other parts of his country. His lines on *The Hudson*, and on *The Battle of Lexington*, are firm and sonorous. *Union and Liberty* is a song that the nation cannot afford to let die.

A large part of Holmes's choicest work consists of short poems, but they are master-pieces of art. The little poem, *The Last Leaf*, has humor, pathos, and the fervor of frankness shifting and blending one into the other as gradually as the change of seasons, yet all subordinate with the modesty of art rather than obtrusive. *The Last Leaf*, so far as it goes, is one of the most perfect productions of American verse. *The Living Temple*, on the other hand, being so physiological, does not in its matter fulfil the promise of the title. A writer, as here, may be hindered as well as aided by the time in which he lives; and though Holmes now and then in the poem breaks through the materializing influence of science, *The Living Temple* is not a poem to be compared with *The Chambered Nautilus.* The latter is as varied as *The Last Leaf,* and has also in its style grace, proportion, and dignity. Not perfect entirely, perhaps : but would that American literature were full of things as good ! It may safely be put side by side with poems of the same length from Shelley or Tennyson ; for it has the rare attributes of life, beauty, and atmosphere.

Holmes possesses the power, which he does not often use, of writing longer poems without being trivial or didactic. *Agnes* is a graceful romance full of charming fancies. *Wind Clouds and Star-Drifts* is another poem that must be considered, in order to do justice to Holmes. In the part entitled "Ambition," the nobler manifestation of that desire is presented. In "*Regrets*" we find traces of what Holmes might have become if he had been purely poet. The whole fancy, in short, is worth a very careful reading.

Holmes, then, is the best of teachers in America to-day in regard to what is true wit and true feeling. He knows his readers; he has made himself acquainted with their desires and their needs. He is also a manly writer; but besides being vigorous and energetic, he is practical and economical enough in the use of his intellectual material to secure from it the largest possible effectiveness. He proves sometimes that he can be an artist in the use of language ; and now and then, if the reader will study him thoroughly, he will find him grappling with the deepest spiritual problems.

Special reference : Holmes's Poems. Houghton, Mifflin, & Co.

ON LENDING A PUNCH-BOWL.

This ancient silver bowl of mine, it tells of good old
    times,
Of joyous days, and jolly nights, and merry Christmas
    chimes ;
They were a free and jovial race, but honest, brave, and
    true,
That dipped their ladle in the punch when this old bowl
    was new.

A Spanish galleon brought the bar ; so runs the ancient
    tale ;
'T was hammered by an Antwerp smith, whose arm was
    like a flail ;
And now and then between the strokes, for fear his
    strength should fail,
He wiped his brow, and quaffed a cup of good old Flem-
    ish ale.

'T was purchased by an English squire, to please his lov-
    ing dame,
Who saw the cherubs, and conceived a longing for the
    same ;
And oft as on the ancient stock another twig was found,
'T was filled with caudle spiced and hot, and handed
    smoking round.

But, changing hands, it reached at length a Puritan
    divine,
Who used to follow Timothy, and take a little wine,
But hated punch and prelacy ; and so it was, perhaps,
He went to Leyden, where he found conventicles and
    schnaps.

And then, of course, you know what 's next,—it left the
    Dutchman's shore
With those that in the *Mayflower* came,—a hundred souls
    and more,—
Along with all the furniture, to fill their new abodes,—
To judge by what is still on hand, at least a hundred l ads.

'T was on a dreary winter's eve, the night was closing
    dim,
When brave Miles Standish took the bowl, and filled it to
    the brim ;
The little Captain stood and stirred the posset with his
    sword,
And all his sturdy men-at-arms were ranged about the
    board.

He poured the fiery Hollands in,—the man that never
    feared,—
He took a long and solemn draught, and wiped his
    yellow beard ;
And one by one the musketeers—the men that fought
    and prayed—
All drank as 't were their mother's milk, and not a man
    afraid.

That night, affrighted from his nest, the screaming eagle
    flew,
He heard the Pequot's [1] ringing whoop, the soldier's wild
    halloo ;
And there the sachem learned the rule he taught to kith
    and kin :
" Run from the white man when you find he smells of
    Hollands gin ! "

[1] *Pequot,* an ancient tribe of Indians in New England.

A hundred years, and fifty more, had spread their leaves
    and snows,
A thousand rubs had flattened down each little cherub's
    nose,
When once again the bowl was filled, but not in mirth or
    joy,
'T was mingled by a mother's hand to cheer her parting
    boy.

Drink, John, she said, 't will do you good,—poor child,
    you 'll never bear
This working in the dismal trench, out in the midnight
    air ;
And if, God bless me !—you were hurt, 't would keep
    away the chill ;
So John *did* drink,—and well he wrought that night at
    Bunker's Hill !

I tell you, there was generous warmth in good old English
    cheer ;
I tell you 't was a pleasant thought to bring its symbol
    here ;
'T is but the fool that loves excess ; hast thou a drunken
    soul ?
Thy bane is in thy shallow skull, not in my silver bowl !

I love the memory of the past,—its pressed yet fragrant
    flowers,—
The moss that clothes its broken walls,—the ivy on its
    towers ;—
Nay, this poor bawble it bequeathed,—my eyes grow
    moist and dim,
To think of all the vanished joys that danced around its
    brim.

7

Then fill a fair and honest cup, and bear it straight to me ;
The goblet hallows all it holds, whate'er the liquid be ;
And may the cherubs on its face protect me from the sin,
That dooms one to those dreadful words : " My dear,
　　where *have* you been ?"

THE LAST LEAF.

I saw him once before,
As he passed by the door,
　　And again
The pavement stones resound,
As he totters o'er the ground
　　With his cane.

They say that in his prime,
Ere the pruning-knife of Time
　　Cut him down,
Not a better man was found
By the Crier [1] on his round
　　Through the town.

But now he walks the streets,
And he looks at all he meets
　　Sad and wan,
And he shakes his feeble head,
That it seems as if he said,
　　" They are gone."

[1] *Crier*, a former official in this country, who gave public notices
by loud proclamation.

The mossy marbles rest
On the lips that he has prest
    In their bloom,
And the names he loved to hear
Have been carved for many a year
    On the tomb.

My grandmamma has said—
Poor old lady, she is dead
    Long ago,
That he had a Roman nose,
And his cheek was like a rose
    In the snow.

But now his nose is thin,
And it rests upon his chin
    Like a staff,
And a crook is in his back,
And a melancholy crack
    In his laugh.

I know it is a sin
For me to sit and grin
    At him here ;
But the old three-cornered hat,
And the breeches, and all that,
    Are so queer !

And if I should live to be
The last leaf upon the tree
    In the spring,
Let them smile as I do now,
At the old forsaken bough
    Where I cling.

THE STETHOSCOPE SONG.

A PROFESSIONAL BALLAD.

There was a young man in Boston town,
　　He bought him a STETHOSCOPE [1] nice and new,
All mounted and finished and polished down,
　　With an ivory cap and a stopper too.

It happened a spider within did crawl,
　　And spun him a web of ample size,
Wherein there chanced one day to fall
　　A couple of very imprudent flies.

The first was a bottle-fly, big and blue,
　　The second was smaller, and thin and long ;
So there was a concert between the two,
　　Like an octave flute and a tavern gong.

Now being from Paris but recently,
　　This fine young man would show his skill ;
And so they gave him, his hand to try,
　　A hospital patient extremely ill.

Some said that his *liver* was short of *bile*,
　　And some that his *heart* was over size,
While some kept arguing all the while
　　He was crammed with *tubercles* up to his eyes.

This fine young man then up stepped he,
　　And all the doctors made a pause ;

---

[1] *Stethoscope*, a medical instrument for learning, by its applicati
to the chest, the condition of internal organs.

Said he,—The man must die, you see,
  By the fifty-seventh of Louis's [1] laws.

But since the case is a desperate one,
  To explore his chest it may be well ;
For if he should die and it were not done,
  You know the *autopsy* would not tell.

Then out his stethoscope he took,
  And on it placed his curious ear ;
Mon Dieu ! said he, with a knowing look,
  Why here is a sound that 's mighty queer !

The *bourdonnement* [2] is very clear,—
  Amphoric buzzing, as I 'm alive !
Five doctors took their turn to hear ;
  Amphoric buzzing, said all the five.

There 's *empyema* beyond a doubt ;
  We 'll plunge a *trocar* [3] in his side,—
The diagnosis was made out,
  They tapped the patient ; so he died.

Now such as hate new-fashioned toys
  Began to look extremely glum ;
They said that *rattles* were made for boys,
  And vowed that his *buzzing* was all a hum.

[1] *Antoine Louis*, a celebrated French surgeon, born at Metz in 1723.

[2] *Bourdonnement*, a buzzing sound like that of an insect.

[3] *Trocar*, a surgical instrument for evacuating fluids from cavities.

There was an old lady had long been sick,
    And what was the matter none did know ;
Her pulse was slow, though her tongue was quick ;
    To her this knowing youth must go.

So there the nice old lady sat,
    With phials and boxes all in a row ;
She asked the young doctor what he was at,
    To thump her and tumble her ruffles so.

Now when the stethoscope came out,
    The flies began to buzz and whiz ;–
O ho ! the matter is clear, no doubt ;
    An *aneurism* there plainly is.

The *bruit de rape*[1] and the *bruit de scie*[1]
    And the *bruit de diable*[1] are all combined ;
How happy Bouillaud[2] would be,
    If he a case like this could find !

Now, when the neighboring doctors found
    A case so rare had been descried,
They every day her ribs did pound
    In squads of twenty ; so she died.

Then six young damsels, slight and frail,
    Received this kind young doctor's cares ;
They all were getting slim and pale,
    And short of breath on mounting stairs.

---

[1] *Bruit de rape,*
Bruit de scie,
Bruit de diable, } The young doctor is alluding to medical symptoms. See *Foster's Medical Dict., Bruit.*

[2] Jean Baptiste Bouillaud, professor of clinics in the Medical Faculty of Paris, born at Angoulême in 1796.

They all made rhymes with " sighs " and " skies,"
  And loathed their puddings and buttered rolls,
And dieted much to their friend's surprise,
  On pickles and pencils and chalk and coals.

So fast their little hearts did bound,
  The frightened insects buzzed the more ;
So over all their chests he found
  The *râle sifflant,*[1] and *râle sonore.*[1]

He shook his head ;—there 's grave disease,—
  I greatly fear you all must die ;
A slight *post-mortem,* if you please,
  Surviving friends would gratify.

The six young damsels wept aloud,
  Which so prevailed on six young men,
That each his honest love avowed,
  Whereat they all got well again.

This poor young man was all aghast ;
  The price of stethoscopes came down ;
And so he was reduced at last
  To practise in a country town.

The doctors being very sore,
  A stethoscope they did devise,
That had a rammer to clear the bore,
  With a knob at the end to kill the flies.

Now use your ears, all you that can,
  But don't forget to mind your eyes,
Or you may be cheated, like this young man,
  By a couple of silly, abnormal flies.

---

[1] *Râle sifflant* ⎱ Other symptoms. See, as before, *Foster's*
  Râle sonore ⎰ *Medical Dict., Râles.*

Summary.

Even though there is still no little difference of opinion on the subject, it may be well to endeavor to form some comparative estimate of the poets in the present group. The poetic attainment of each may not differ much in rank from that of any other, and yet it may be of advantage to inquire into their individual merits.

Can we say that among these poets Poe holds the first place? So far from this being true, it may be doubted with good grounds whether any one of the others were not more a poet than he. It would be incorrect, however, to reach this conclusion, as has sometimes been done, by alleging merely his deficiency in grasp of the social and political needs of the community; it is rather because his lines usually lack the element of feeling, which is almost an essential in good poetry.

Unlike Poe, Emerson, at his best, has feeling of a high quality, yet Emerson's best verse is a very small part of his verse; and, after all, Emerson is chiefly an essayist.

Bryant is more even. He will bear careful study, and is, possibly, for one who wishes to train himself in the art of versification, the finest model[1] among all those poets who were his congeners. Yet Bryant's song is hardly ever heard when he comes out of his woods; he is not distinctively a poet of human society.

---

[1] Longfellow, who is broader and stronger, is probably not so excellent a model for the student.

The question may be asked, in this connection, how among the others Holmes stands? In a writer of such perennial vigor, who is still living, it is happily too early to estimate his performance; but his humor makes him far from the least memorable of the group.

As to Whittier, his merit over Bryant is that he has more passion. His fault, if it be one, is that he is partisan.

Jones Very has a place and consideration apart. His spiritual poise of mind, however, would seem to place him above Whittier, while his lack of poetic observation on the real world of men would prevent him from being named as the equal of Lowell or Longfellow.

Lowell, on the other hand, has throughout his life been among men, and has made his writings a part of their lives. Scarcely a poem, or, indeed, a prose writing of his, but shows his genius; a genius not only large and versatile, but sane in its influence, and when stopping a moment to jest, at once serious again. Yet Lowell has not such art as Longfellow; he is a great man writing poetry, rather than a poet pure and simple.

Longfellow has the imagination of the fireside. He has sung songs of home, or told homely stories of distant lands that are favorites the world over. So familiar has he become, that there is hardly any one of education, at least in this country, who has not felt his influence. Such a one must indeed be a poet of a large part of human life, one to whom has been granted a deep and thorough vision of humanity.

Yet none of these, if we compare them with the foremost in history, is fairly entitled to be called a great poet. For the execution reached here has been hardly more than lyric; beyond this compass lie the drama and the epic with their fierce play and heat of passion, which American poets thus far have hardly touched.

2. (*For the three following poets, cf. under the general introduction to " Contemporaries."*)

WALT WHITMAN.

Walt Whitman's songs, as he calls them, have not the technical requirements of poetry ; on the other hand, his rhythmical lines have sometimes in their content and in their style certain poetical qualities to an unusual degree.

Walt Whitman was born at West Hills, Long Island, New York, May 31, 1819. He went to school in New York City, and learned also the printers' and carpenters' trades. Later, he taught school, edited newspapers, was a hospital nurse in the war of 1861, and afterwards became a government clerk at Washington. During his life he travelled extensively on foot through the United States.

For the magnitude of his vision Whitman owes much to Homer, to Shakespeare, and to the Book of Job. He was also largely influenced by Emerson's essays, whose independence and exaggeration he has imitated. The most important source for his genius is his observation of American barbarism, as he terms it. He embodies his sense of this in vivid imagery; imagining frequently and boldly that America and himself possess the same traits,—pride, carelessness, and generous receptivity.

The subjects of Whitman's verse are the great elemental forces of nature,—the sound of the sea, the lapse of time, or the blaze of the sun; the United States with its men, trades, and cities; and the experience of the author, as he wanders out-of-doors, great-hearted in his sentiment for men.

Certain of Whitman's poems are deservedly famous: notably those on President Lincoln, *O Captain, My Captain*, and *When Lilacs Last in the Dooryard Bloomed; O Star of France*; and among passages there is almost a visible splendor in that part of the *Song of Myself*, beginning " I understand the large hearts of heroes," and including the description of the rescuing ship, of the slave, and of the fireman; and in the lines following, which tell the story of the sea-fight.

The fact that Whitman is a poet who excels by passages, makes it specially fit to select his shortest poems, which are found most nearly to fulfil the artistic conditions of proportion and unity. It may be observed, also, that these poems are not widely open to charges of extravagance. As to their several species, some are simple, gentle, loving, as *The First Dandelion, The Ship Starting, Sometimes with One I Love, What Think You I Take my Pen in Hand? Recorders, Ages Hence.* Others are full of manly disdain,—*To a Certain Civilian* and *Not Youth Pertains to Me*, with its half serious close :—

"Beauty, knowledge, inure not to me,—yet there are
    two or three things inure to me,
I have nourish'd the wounded and sooth'd many a
    dying soldier,
And at intervals waiting or in the midst of camp
    composed these songs."

Some are descriptive with ideal truth underneath, such as *I saw Old General at Bay*, and *Delicate Cluster.* Others, again, display fancy, as *The Dying Veteran*, and *Yonnondio*, the last ending impressively; and one, at least, *Aboard at a Ship's Helm*, has imagination.

Whitman had a mind of great power,—so far he ought to have the homage that he has received at home as well as from abroad. Still we may be not less firm in believing, on account of his disregard of the broad canons of literary form, and still more of ideas, that praise of him should be moderate, although, with less disdain of literary form he would certainly have been a much larger and more important figure in American literature than he can now be considered.

THE FIRST DANDELION.

Simple and fresh and fair from winter's close emerging,
As if no artifice of fashion, business, politics, had ever
    been,
Forth from its sunny nook of shelter'd grass—innocent,
    golden, calm as the dawn,
The spring's first dandelion shows its trustful face.

THE SHIP STARTING.

Lo, the unbounded sea,
On its breast a ship starting, spreading all sails, carrying
even her moonsails,
The pennant is flying aloft as she speeds she speeds so
stately—below emulous waves press forward,
They surround the ship with shining curving motions
and foam.

WHAT THINK YOU I TAKE MY PEN IN HAND?

What think you I take my pen in hand to record?
The battle-ship, perfect-model'd, majestic, that I saw pass
the offing to-day under full sail?
The splendors of the past day? or the splendor of the
night that envelops me?
Or the vaunted glory and growth of the great city spread
around me?—no;
But merely of two simple men I saw to-day on the pier in
the midst of the crowd, parting the parting of dear
friends,
The one to remain hung on the other's neck and passionately kiss'd him,
While the one to depart tightly prest the one to remain in
his arms.

SOMETIMES WITH ONE I LOVE.

Sometimes with one I love I fill myself with rage for fear
I effuse unreturn'd love,
But now I think there is no unreturn'd love, the pay is
certain one way or another,
(I loved a certain person ardently and my love was not
return'd,
Yet out of that I have written these songs.)

RECORDERS AGES HENCE.

Recorders ages hence,
Come, I will take you down underneath this impassive
    exterior, I will tell you what to say of me,
Publish my name and hand up my picture as that of the
    tenderest lover,
The friend the lover's portrait, of whom his friend his
    lover was fondest,
Who was not proud of his songs, but of the measureless
    ocean of love within him, and freely pour'd it
    forth,
Who often walk'd lonesome walks thinking of his dear
    friends, his lovers,
Who pensive away from one he lov'd often lay sleepless
    and dissatisfied at night,
Who knew too well the sick, sick dread lest the one he
    lov'd might secretly be indifferent to him,
Whose happiest days were far away through fields, in
    woods, on hills, he and another wandering, hand in
    hand, they twain apart from other men,
Who oft as he saunter'd the streets curv'd with his arm
    the shoulder of his friend, while the arm of his
    friend rested upon him also.

TO A CERTAIN CIVILIAN.

Did you ask dulcet rhymes from me?
Did you seek the civilian's peaceful and languishing
    rhymes?
Did you find what I sang erewhile so hard to follow?
Why I was not singing erewhile for you to follow, to un-
    derstand,—nor am I now;
(I have been born of the same as the war was born,

The drum-corps' rattle is ever to me sweet music, I love
 well the martial dirge,
With slow wail and convulsive throb leading the officer's
 funeral ;)
What to such as you anyhow such a poet as I ? therefore leave my works,
And go lull yourself with what you can understand, and
 with piano-tunes,
For I lull nobody, and you will never understand me.

NOT YOUTH PERTAINS TO ME.

Not youth pertains to me,
Nor delicatesse, I cannot beguile the time with talk,
Awkward in the parlor, neither a dancer nor elegant,
In the learn'd coterie sitting constrain'd and still, for
 learning inures not to me,
Beauty, knowledge, inure not to me—yet there are two or
 three things inure to me,
I have nourish'd the wounded and sooth'd many a dying
 soldier,
And at intervals waiting, or in the midst of camp,
Composed these songs.

I SAW OLD GENERAL AT BAY.

I saw old General at bay,
(Old as he was, his gray eyes yet shone out in battle like
 stars),
His small force was now completely hemm'd in, in his
 works,
He call'd for volunteers to run the enemy's lines, a desperate emergency,

I saw a hundred and more step forth from the ranks, but
    two or three were selected,
I saw them receive their orders aside, they listen'd with
    care, the adjutant was very grave,
I saw them depart with cheerfulness, freely risking their
    lives.

DELICATE CLUSTER.

Delicate cluster ! flag of teeming life !
Covering all my lands—all my sea-shores lining !
Flag of death ! (how I watch'd you through the smoke of
    battle pressing !
How I heard you flap and rustle, cloth defiant !)
Flag cerulean—sunny flag, with the orbs of night dappled !
Ah my silvery beauty—ah my woolly white and crimson !
Ah to sing the song of you, my matron mighty !
My sacred one, my mother.

THE DYING VETERAN.

(A Long Island incident—early part of the present century.)

Amid these days of order, ease, prosperity,
Amid the current songs of beauty, peace, decorum,
I cast a reminiscence (likely 't will offend you,
I heard it in my boyhood ;)—More than a generation
    since,
A queer old savage man, a fighter under Washington
    himself,
(Large, brave, cleanly, hot-blooded, no talker, rather
    spiritualistic,
Had fought in the ranks—fought well—had been all
    through the Revolutionary war,)

Lay dying—sons, daughters, church-deacons, lovingly
    tending him,
Sharping their sense, their ears, towards his murmuring,
    half-caught words :
" Let me return again to my war-days,
To the lights and scenes—to forming the line of battle,
To the scouts ahead reconnoitering,
To the cannons, the grim artillery ;
To the galloping aids, carrying orders,
To the wounded, the fallen, the heat, the suspense,
The perfume strong, the smoke, the deafening noise ;
Away with your life of peace !—your joys of peace !
Give me my old wild battle-life again ! "

YONNONDIO.

(The sense of the word is *lament for the aborigines*.   It is an Iro-
quois term, and has been used for a personal name.)

A song, a poem of itself—the word itself a dirge,
Amid the wilds, the rocks, the storm and wintry night,
To me such misty, strange tableaux the syllables calling
    up ;
Yonnondio—I see, far in the west or north, a limitless
    ravine, with plains and mountains dark,
I see swarms of stalwart chieftains, medicine-men, and
    warriors,
As flitting by like clouds of ghosts, they pass and are
    gone in the twilight,
(Race of the woods, the landscapes free, and the falls !
No picture, poem, statement, passing them to the future :)
Yonnondio !   Yonnondio !—unlimn'd they disappear ;
To-day gives place and fades—the cities, farms, factories
    fade :

A muffled sonorous sound, a wailing word is borne
    through the air for a moment,
Then blank and gone and still, and utterly lost.

ABOARD AT A SHIP'S HELM.

Aboard at a ship's helm,
A young steersman steering with care.

Through fog on a sea-coast dolefully ringing,
An ocean bell—O a warning bell, rock'd by the waves.

O, you give good notice indeed, you bell by the sea-
    reefs ringing,
Ringing, ringing, to warn the ship from its wreck-place.

For as on the alert, O steersman, you mind the loud
    admonition,
The bows turn, the freighted ship tacking speeds away
    under her gray sails,
The beautiful and noble ship with all her precious wealth
    speeds away gayly and safe.

But O the ship, the immortal ship! O ship aboard the
    ship!
Ship of the body, ship of the soul, voyaging, voyaging,
    voyaging.

BAYARD TAYLOR.

The career of Bayard Taylor possesses both an historical and a personal interest. It is worth while to note, in passing, the historical interest of his work, even through those of his literary efforts which were not a complete success, because in some of his productions of this nature he was chiefly a pioneer, as in his plays, his novels, and in a portion of his lyrics. Others of his shorter poems have a greater literary worth, because they exhibit Taylor himself, who, as a writer, was, above everything else, sincere. These shorter poems are chiefly on the subject of love, though occasionally the poems of a traveller.

Bayard Taylor was born at Kennet Square, Penn., January 11, 1825. In 1842 he became apprentice to a printer; in 1844–45 made a pedestrian tour in Europe; in 1849 visited California, and in 1851 set out on his first tour through the East. During the succeeding ten years he made various long journeys, descriptions of which were given in a series of spirited and informing books of travel. He did good work for journals, principally for the *New York Tribune*. He died December 19, 1878, in Berlin, to which capital he had been appointed minister from the United

States. At the time of his death he was engaged
upon a life of Goethe.

Of his lyric poems, which are the most interesting,
The Poet in the East is one of Taylor's happiest con-
ceits. The rhythm is delicate, the imagination attended by fancy, and the mood and place close to
the poet's heart. Of kindred love poems, *On the Sea*
well suggests the poetic influence of night on the
water, and *Proposal* is characterized by a strong
abruptness. *True Love's Time of Day* could have
been written by no one but a man of exceeding sen-
sitiveness. *Possession* is firm in its love fancies. The
Bedouin Song has been popular, but it is of a cheaper
texture than the others. In his poems on love, it is
the confidence and presumption of that passion that
Taylor expresses, not its shrinking and bashfulness.
Among poems on other subjects, *Hassan to His
Mare* would be an ideal expression of love for a pet
animal, were it not marred by the close of the second stanza; while the lines *On Leaving California*
could not have been truer to California feeling. Into
his lesser lyrics he infused a warmth and richness of
color which is drawn from his own healthy nature,
and which heightened the glow of his work. His
odes are talented performances; the *Centennial Ode*
is something more; but in none of them has he
shown such special adaptation, as was possessed by
Lowell, for this kind of poetry.

The *Picture of St. John* and *Lars*, though not
well known, are by no means failures. Assuredly,
a long poem as successfully sustained as the former
is must always command respect from persons of

poetic taste ; and all through it Taylor shows that he had really lived in and breathed the art atmosphere of Italy. *Lars* opens with a classic carefulness and beauty in its suggestive descriptions. The picture of Brita is nobly done. As a whole the poem is unequal and rather long, but in the better parts has sturdiness and originality. The translation of *Faust* should be mentioned because it has been ranked with the great translations of literature, and could have been produced only by a writer who possessed, with poetic understanding, original power.

Taylor has not proved to posterity that he was a man of genius. That he had poetic taste and talent, however, to an unusual degree is indubitable. A greater poet would have combined the grace and severity of the New England school with Taylor's free and democratic sympathy for many styles and subjects. Yet Taylor, besides being a representative in poetry of certain parts of the American genius, remains an historic figure as a man of letters.

THE POET IN THE EAST.

The Poet came to the Land of the East,
  When spring was in the air :
The Earth was dressed for a wedding feast,
  So young she seemed, and fair ;
And the Poet knew the Land of the East,—
  His soul was native there.

All things to him were the visible forms
  Of early and precious dreams,—

Familiar visions that mocked his quest
    Beside the Western streams,
Or gleamed in the gold of the clouds, unrolled
    In the sunset's dying beams.

He looked above in the cloudless calm,
    And the Sun sat on his throne ;
The breath of gardens, deep in balm,
    Was all about him blown,
And a brother to him was the princely Palm,
    For he cannot live alone.

His feet went forth on the myrtled hills,
    And the flowers their welcome shed ;
The meads of milk-white asphodel
    They knew the Poet's tread,
And far and wide, in a scarlet tide,
    The poppy's bonfire spread.

And, half in shade and half in sun,
    The Rose sat in her bower,
With a passionate thrill in her crimson heart—
    She had waited for the hour !
And, like a bride's, the Poet kissed
    The lips of the glorious flower.

Then, the Nightingale, who sat above
    In the boughs of the citron-tree,
Sang : We are no rivals, brother mine,
    Except in minstrelsy ;
For the rose you kissed with the kiss of love
    Is faithful still to me.

And further sang the Nightingale :
   Your bower not distant lies.
I heard the sound of a Persian lute
   From the jasmined window rise,
And, twin-bright stars, through the lattice-bars,
   I saw the Sultana's eyes.

The Poet said : I will here abide,
   In the Sun's unclouded door ;
Here are the wells of all delight
   On the lost Arcadian shore :
Here is the light on sea and land,
   And the dream deceives no more.

ON LEAVING CALIFORNIA.

O fair young land, the youngest, fairest far
   Of which our world can boast,—
Whose guardian planet, Evening's silver star
   Illumes thy golden coast,—

How art thou conquered, tamed in all the pride
   Of savage beauty still !
How brought, O panther of the splendid hide,
   To know thy master's will !

No more thou sittest on thy tawny hills
   In indolent repose ;
Or pour'st the crystal of a thousand rills
   Down from the house of snows.

But where the wild oats wrapped thy knees in gold,
  The plowman drives his share,
And where, through cañons deep, thy streams are rolled,
  The miner's arm is bare.

Yet in thy lap, thus rudely rent and torn,
  A nobler seed shall be :
Mother of mighty men, thou shalt not mourn
  Thy lost virginity ;

Thy human children shall restore the grace
  Gone with thy fallen pines :
The wild, barbaric beauty of thy face
  Shall round to classic lines.

And Order, Justice, Social Law shall curb
  Thy untamed energies ;
And Art and Science, with their dreams superb,
  Replace thine ancient ease.

The marble, sleeping in thy mountains now,
  Shall live in sculptures rare ;
Thy native oak shall crown the sage's brow,—
  Thy bay, the poet's hair.

Thy tawny hills shall bleed their purple wine,
  Thy valleys yield their oil ;
And Music, with her eloquence divine,
  Persuade thy sons to toil.

Till Hesper, as he trims his silver beam,
  No happier land shall see,
And earth shall find her old Arcadian dream
  Restored again in thee.

SIDNEY LANIER.

Among the American poets of the younger generation who have passed away during the last thirty years, no one deserves higher encomium than Lanier. Materially, fate pinched him, but whether oppressed by misfortune or cheered by success, he never lost the poetic fire within.

Sidney Lanier was born at Macon, Georgia, February 3, 1842. His earliest poems are not among his best; although some of his verse in dialect exhibits a humor which was repressed in his later literary production, and *Nirvana* is more successful in seriousness than is often the case with an early poem by a celebrated author.

There is something about the verse of Lanier—defective as his performance is,—for it must be acknowledged that he was not always equal in clearness and literary judgment,—that inspires respect from every lover of genius. Even where he was not perfect, he showed, as in *Corn*, that he had grasped firmly the distinction in poetics between the small and the great. Beside this rare attainment, or gift, whichever it was, Lanier, even in early work, had reached a power of imagination that may be com-

pared not unfavorably with that of Longfellow between his thirty-third and thirty-seventh years ; in the
minor matters of verbal imagination and onomato-
pœia Lanier was at times greatly Longfellow's
superior.

Lanier's merits as a poet are numerous and con-
siderable. A large nature like his could not express
itself trivially or in narrow limits. He has done well
in the treatment of love, philosophy, mysticism,
socialism, in the ballad, and technically in melody
and harmony of rhythm.

This is not to say that he has excelled in all points
alike or equally. *My Springs* is one of Lanier's most
beautiful love songs ; its subject is not, as a general
thing, too commonly or too well treated. Lanier's
work elsewhere is full of the tenderest love passages.
Yet it is not in dealing with love that he is pre-
eminent.

Nor is it so on the dubious ground of poetry
carrying a philosophical message. Here Lanier is at
fault not only from the possibly inherent difficulty
of such themes, but because of his own lack of special study in this direction. *Clover* is one of the
plainest of these didactic poems; but in this as in
others, is obtruded too conscious alliteration.

So, too, in Lanier's employment of mysticism.
There is really no good reason, theoretically or prac-
tically, why a mystical subject is not suitable for
poetry, provided only the obstacles be surmounted.
Lanier's *Acknowledgment* is of that sort of mysticism
which when uttered with any fulness in poetry is
always deserving of esteem ; even though Lanier, or

any other American poet, has not yet adjusted poetry to the satisfactory reflection of abstract religious thought.

It is in the deep music of Lanier's line that his greatness is to be found. Compare the *Symphony*, the *Revenge of Hamish*, or the *Marshes of Glynn* with the best previous American verse; say Longfellow's *Evangeline* or *Hiawatha*, Lowell's *Commemoration Ode*, and Whittier's *Barbara Frietchie*. In harmony of sound, I believe, Lanier should have the preference; he was a musician primarily, they were not. That the knack of music in poetry is less important than the perfect expression of the finest and noblest ideas, makes him on the whole their inferior. Even so, he marks an epoch in American verse that makes his position unique, exceptional, and historic. For poetry at its highest worth must not only consist of the best ideas and conceptions, but must flow in the best rhythm. Yet the best rhythm is not easy or frequent. It exists as an art only seldom in a language. The best rhythm has depth; it underlies the line rather than floats on its surface. Its masters in English verse are in the foremost place, the Elizabethan dramatists; also Milton, and secondarily Tennyson. Pope or Dryden did not have it; they had rather the knack of a grasshopper-like metre that skips jerkily forth here and there. No one of American poets previous to Lanier possessed fully the stronger rhythm. Lanier has it, not perhaps at its virile best, and often mixed with something artificial from his own preconceptions; but he has it after all now and then, and has it clearly and strongly.

Lanier's line is generous. There are deep places in it; the reader takes a long breath, for the poet prefers not only the amplitude of the pentameter, but often adds an additional syllable.

In the development of his verse, Lanier finds many new harmonics. The *Marshes of Glynn* shows almost a coloring of sound. This poem, as others of Lanier's, is a work of imagination, and deals not only with single shapes, but with masses. *Tampa Robbins* is a vivid study also of musical sensation. The *Revenge of Hamish* is, perhaps, to be placed higher than the *Symphony* and the rest of Lanier's poems, on account of its force, its concreteness, its verbal imagination, and its vigorous style.

After years of protracted struggle with a vital malady, Lanier died at Lynn, N. C., Sept. 7, 1881. As he was then only thirty-nine, but had still shown pre-eminent individual attainment, his powers, it may be fairly assumed, had not reached their full height. The little poem, *Opposition*, indicates what might have been the outcome, morally, in his verse. He was naturally hopeful, but as far from shallow optimism as from shallow pessimism. His own physical and intellectual pain afforded him experience which was transmuted into sympathy for the suffering of others. For himself, he was triumphantly joyous through his own trials; while for others he knew that bitter compassion that perplexes while it sustains the best Christianity of to-day.

Special References: Lanier's Poetical Works, with an introduction by W. H. Ward. Chas. Scribner's Sons.

THE REVENGE OF HAMISH.

It was three slim does and a ten-tined buck in the
    bracken lay ;
  And all of a sudden the sinister smell of a man,
  Awaft on a wind-shift, wavered and ran
Down the hill-side and sifted along through the bracken
    and passed that way.

Then Nan got a-tremble at nostril ; she was the dainti-
    est doe ;
  In the print of her velvet flank on the velvet fern
  She reared, and rounded her ears in turn.
Then the buck leapt up, and his head as a king's to a
    crown did go.

Full high in the breeze, and he stood as if Death had
    the form of a deer ;
  And the two slim does long lazily stretching arose,
  For their day-dream slowlier came to a close,
Till they woke and were still, breath-bound with wait-
    ing and wonder and fear.

Then Alan the huntsman sprang over the hillock, the
    hounds shot by,
  The does and the ten-tined buck made a marvellous
    bound,
  The hounds swept after with never a sound,
But Alan loud winded his horn in sign that the quarry
    was nigh.

For at dawn of that day proud Maclean of Lochbuy to
    the hunt had waxed wild,
  And he cursed at old Alan till Alan fared off with
    the hounds

For to drive him the deer to the lower glen-grounds :
" I will kill a red deer " quoth Maclean, " in the sight of
the wife and the child."

So gayly he paced with the wife and the child to his
chosen stand ;
But he hurried tall Hamish the henchman ahead :
" Go turn,"
Cried Maclean—" if the deer seek to cross to the burn,
Do thou turn them to me : nor fail, lest thy back be as
red as thy hand."

Now hard-fortuned Hamish, half blown of his breath
with the height of the hill,
Was white in the face when the ten-tined buck and the
does
Drew leaping to burn-ward ; huskily rose
His shouts and his nether lip twitched, and his legs
were o'er-weak for his will.

So the deer darted lightly by Hamish and bounded away
to the burn.
But Maclean never bating his watch tarried waiting
below.
Still Hamish hung heavy with fear for to go
All the space of an hour ; then he went, and his face was
greenish and stern,

And his eye sat back in the socket, and shrunken the eye-
balls shone,
As withdrawn from a vision of deeds it were shame to
see.

" Now, now, grim henchman, what is 't with thee ? "
Brake Maclean, and his wrath rose red as a beacon the
    wind hath upblown.

" Three does and a ten-tined buck made out," spoke
    Hamish, full mild,
  " And I ran for to turn, but my breath it was blown,
    and they passed ;
  I was weak, for ye called ere I broke me my fast."
Cried Maclean : " Now a ten-tined buck in the sight of
    the wife and the child

I had killed if the gluttonous kern had not wrought me a
    snail's own wrong ! "
  Then he sounded and down came kinsmen and clans-
    men all :
  " Ten blows, for ten tine, on his back let fall,
And reckon no stroke if the blood follow not the bite of
    the thong ! "

So Hamish made bare, and took him his strokes ; at the
    last he smiled.
  " Now I 'll to the burn," quoth Maclean, " for it still
    may be,
  If a slimmer-paunched henchman will hurry with me,
I shall kill me the ten-tined buck for a gift to the wife
    and the child ! "

Then the clansmen departed, by this path and that ; and
    over the hill
  Sped Maclean with an onward wrath for an inward
    shame ;

And that place of the lashing full quiet became ;
And the wife and the child stood sad ; and blood-backed
    Hamish sat still.

But look ! red Hamish has risen ; quick about and about
    turns he.
  "There is none betwixt me and the crag-top ! " he
    screams under breath.
Then, livid as Lazarus lately from death,
He snatches the child from the mother, and clambers the
    crag toward the sea.

Now the mother drops breath ; she is dumb, and her
    heart goes dead for a space,
  Till the motherhood, mistress of death, shrieks,
    shrieks through the glen,
And that place of the lashing is live with men,
And Maclean, and the gillie that told him, dash up in a
    desperate race.

Not a breath's time for asking ; an eye-glance reveals
    all the tale untold.
  They follow mad Hamish afar up the crag toward the
    sea,
  And the lady cries : "Clansmen, run for a fee !—
Yon castle and lands to the two first hands that shall
    hook him and hold

Fast Hamish back from the brink ! "—and ever she flies
    up the steep,
  And the clansmen pant, and they sweat, and they
    jostle and strain.

9

But, mother, 't is vain ; but, father, 't is vain ;
Stern Hamish stands bold on the brink, and dangles the
child o'er the deep.

Now a faintness falls on the men that run, and they all
stand still.
And the wife prays Hamish as if he were God, on her
knees,
Crying : "Hamish ! O Hamish ! but please, but
please
For to spare him ! " and Hamish still dangles the child,
with a wavering will.

On a sudden he turns ; with a sea-hawk scream, and a
gibe, and a song,
Cries : "So ; I will spare ye the child if, in sight of ye
all,
Ten blows on Maclean's bare back shall fall,
And ye reckon no stroke if the blood follow not at the
bite of the thong ! "

Then Maclean he set hardly his tooth to his lip that his
tooth was red,
Breathed short for a space, said : " Nay, but it never
shall be !
Let me hurl off the damnable hound in the sea ! "
But the wife : "Can Hamish go fish us the child from
the sea, if dead ?

Say yea !—Let them lash *me*, Hamish ? "—" Nay ! "—
" Husband, the lashing will heal ;
But, oh, who will heal me the bonny sweet bairn in his
grave ?

Could ye cure me my heart with the death of a
knave ?
Quick ! love ! I will bare thee—so—kneel ! " Then
Maclean 'gan slowly to kneel

With never a word, till presently downward he jerked to
the earth.
Then the henchman—he that smote Hamish—would
tremble and lag ;
"Strike, hard ! " quoth Hamish, full stern, from the
crag ;
Then he struck him, and "One ! " sang Hamish, and
danced with the child in his mirth.

And no man spake beside Hamish ; he counted each
stroke with a song.
When the last stroke fell, then he moved him a pace
down the height,
And he held forth the child in the heartaching
sight
Of the mother, and looked all pitiful grave, as repenting
a wrong.

And there as the motherly arms stretched out with the
thanksgiving prayer—
And there as the mother crept up with a fearful swift
pace,
Till her finger nigh felt of the bairnie's face—
In a flash fierce Hamish turned round and lifted the
child in the air,

And sprang with the child in his arms from the horrible
height in the sea,

Shrill screeching, " Revenge ! " in the wind-rush ; and
  pallid Maclean,
Age-feeble with anger and impotent pain,
Crawled up on the crag, and lay flat, and locked hold of
  dead roots of a tree—

And gazed hungrily o'er, and the blood from his back
  drip—dripped in the brine,
  And a sea-hawk flung down a skeleton fish as he
  flew,
  And the mother stared white on the waste of blue,
And the wind drove a cloud to seaward, and the sun
  began to shine.

SONG OF THE CHATTAHOOCHEE.

Out of the hills of Habersham,
Down the valleys of Hall,
I hurry amain to reach the plain,
Run the rapid and leap the fall,
Split at the rock and together again,
Accept my bed, or narrow or wide
And flee from folly on every side
With a lover's pain to attain the plain
Far from the hills of Habersham,
Far from the valleys of Hall.

All down the hills of Habersham,
All through the valleys of Hall,
The rushes cried *Abide, abide,*
The wilful waterweed held me thrall,
The laving laurel turned my tide,
The ferns and the fondling grass said *Stay,*

The dewberry dipped for to work delay,
And the little reeds sighed *Abide, abide,*
Here in the hills of Habersham,
Here in the valleys of Hall.

High o'er the hills of Habersham,
Veiling the valleys of Hall,
The hickory told me manifold
Fair tales of shade, the poplar tall
Wrought me her shadowy self to hold,
The chestnut, the oak, the walnut, the pine,
Overleaning with flickering meaning and sign,
Said : *Pass not, so cold, these manifold,*
Deep shades of the hills of Habersham,
These glades in the valleys of Hall.

And oft in the hills of Habersham,
And oft in the valleys of Hall,
The white quartz shone, and the smooth brook-stone
Did bar me of passage with friendly brawl,
And many a luminous jewel lone—
Crystals clear or a cloud with mist
Ruby, garnet, and amethyst—
Made lures with the lights of streaming stone
In the cleft of the hills of Habersham,
In the beds of the valleys of Hall.

But oh, not the hills of Habersham,
And oh, not the valleys of Hall,
Avail; I am fain for to water the plain.
Downward the voices of Duty call—
Downward, to toil and be mixed with the main,
The dry fields burn, and the mills are to turn,

And a myriad flowers mortally yearn,
And the lordly main from beyond the plain
Calls o'er the hills of Habersham,
Calls through the valleys of Hall.

TAMPA ROBINS.[1]

The robin laughed in the orange-tree :
" Ho, windy North, a fig for thee :
While breasts are red and wings are bold
And green trees wave us globes of gold,
Time's scythe shall reap but bliss for me
—Sunlight, song, and the orange-tree.

" Burn, golden globes in leafy sky,
My orange-planets : crimson I
Will shine and shoot among the spheres
(Blithe meteor that no mortal fears)
And thrid the heavenly orange-tree
With orbits bright of minstrelsy.

" If that I hate wild winter's spite—
The gibbet trees, the world in white,
The sky but gray wind over a grave—
Why should I ache, the season's slave ?
I 'll sing from the top of the orange-tree
Gramercy, winter's tyranny.

" I 'll south with the sun and keep my clime ;
My wing is king of the summer-time ;
My breast to the sun his torch shall hold ;
And I 'll call down through the green and gold
Time, take thy scythe, reap bliss for me,
Bestir thee under the orange-tree."

[1] *Tampa*, a bay on the west side of Florida.

PART II.

1. Forerunners.

In a brief general survey of the field of what I will call præ-classic American literature, discussion of that portion containing the works of writers of the seventeenth and eighteenth centuries can hardly be either interesting in itself or fertile in its results. Among the commonplace of those times, a gleam of personality appeared only occasionally in poetry, as in a lyric of Freneau's like *The Wild Honeysuckle*.

It is different with authors during the first generation in the nineteenth century. In the rarity of the intellectual atmosphere, literature was still beginning to form. In prose, Irving and Cooper had originated American fiction. In poetry, Bryant, both by example and by precept, was pointing the way onward, though Bryant's early development in poetic art makes it necessary to consider him not here but among the "Classics."

Other producers of verse at this time were quite various in merit. Very few of them left a lasting name, and are principally interesting historically. Some of them, such as Sprague and Neal, are now indeed nothing more than names. Others are more

fortunate through possessing associations which en-
able their fame to survive. R. H. Dana was formerly
called a critic and a poet; he is now known as
Bryant's friend, and as one of those who had the
best poetical judgment among the men of his time.
Drake wrote *The American Flag* and *The Culprit
Fay*; but we seem to know more of the man himself by reading concerning him his associate Halleck's
memorial lines. Percival will be far more likely to
be remembered through Lowell's essay on *Percival*
than by all the poetry he himself ever wrote. Such
are a few of the attitudes with which Time surveys
those writers who in their own day had been greeted
with loud applause!

Two of the "Forerunners," however, have left a
fame that is more than shadowy. Here the men
behind the works come out distinctly as literary
figures; and the name of each stands for a personality that is quite remarkable. The first of the two,
in point of time as well as of poetic ability, Fitz-
Greene Halleck, was the finest and most typical poet
of that day.[1] In collaboration with Drake he printed
in 1819, under the title of *The Croakers*, a series of
poetical satires upon public characters of the period,
a series which achieved an immediate local fame; but
Halleck is now better known by *Marco Bozzaris* and
Burns. His own character may still better keep him
a lasting name. He lacked, however, the intellectual
independence and the creative genius which is un-
hindered by the wearing and destructive effect of
drudgery. The other writer, Willis, was a man of

[1] Bryant is a poet of the century.

definite and, on the whole, pleasing personality, a man whose light, chatty manner covered a heart and a will that made him a favorite; but Willis, still less than Halleck, had the genius which constitutes a great writer.

A strong extrinsic interest and importance, however, attaches to the group as a whole; in them, better than in those writers whose works are more read by posterity,—Bryant, Longfellow, Lowell, and their compeers,—are seen the unfavorable and deteriorating literary conditions in this country during the first half of the century. The "Forerunners" show, for example, what the consequences were, of writers in the earlier part of the century not finding letters alone sufficient for a livelihood. For it may be observed that the "Forerunners" preferred, instead of the letters, the livelihood; whereas, it may be said, that among the "Classics," Poe, who lived during this period, preferred, as seen by his suffering and death, instead of the livelihood, the letters. Another disadvantage was that foreign influences, especially imitation of foreign models, were too strong as compared with native inspiration; and this ill wind blew no good, so far as independent thought was concerned, to the writers of either group.

Since, therefore, no writer of this group escaped the literary disadvantages of that time, a study of the group, while interesting in itself, will also dispel the glamor which, hanging over the success of the "Classics," hides the difficulties under which the members of the latter group contended and which they so largely overcame; and it will justly be in-

ferred that the " Classics," too, must have been ham-
pered and prevented from attaining a greater height.
And if the study of the " Forerunners " enables a student to realize this fact, it will have done no slight
thing ; for it will have opened his eyes to the truth
that genius is exposed to at least as many difficulties as talent, and will lead him a long way from a
merely admiring view of renowned poets to a critical
consideration of their permanent value as modified
by the time and conditions in which they lived.

PHILIP FRENEAU.

Philip Freneau was the most distinguished poet of the revolutionary time. He was born at New York, January 2, 1752, and was a graduate of Princeton College. Part of his life was spent in journalism and book-writing, part of it on the sea. He served with conspicuous patriotism in the army during the Revolution, during which he was taken prisoner. Freneau found a subject for his verse in his personal knowledge of the war. He died near Freehold, N. J., December 18, 1832.

Freneau is of interest as one of the first poets in America to show signs of personality in literary style. His verse in general may also be studied as helping to the knowledge of the literary conditions of the time, and as showing the crudity of taste then that was, however, mitigated somewhat by the study here and there of the eighteenth-century poets of England.

THE WILD HONEYSUCKLE.

Fair flower, that dost so comely grow,
   Hid in this silent, dull retreat,
Untouched thy honied blossoms blow,
   Unseen thy little branches greet ;

No roving foot shall crush thee here,
No busy hand provoke a tear.

By Nature's self in white arrayed,
  She bade thee shun the vulgar eye,
And planted here the guardian shade,
  And sent soft waters murmuring by ;
  Thus quietly thy summer goes,
  Thy days declining to repose.

Smit with those charms, that must decay,
  I grieve to see thy future doom ;
They died—nor were those flowers more gay,
  The flowers that did in Eden bloom ;
  Unpitying frosts and Autumn's power,
  Shall leave no vestige of this flower.

From morning suns and evening dews,
  At first thy little being came ;
If nothing once, you nothing lose,
  For when you die you are the same ;
  The space between is but an hour,
  The frail duration of a flower.

RICHARD HENRY DANA.

Richard Henry Dana was one of the earliest lovers of poetry in this country who at the same time wrote good poetry himself. Dana was born at Cambridge, Mass., August 15, 1787. He entered Harvard, and later practised law. In childhood he had acquired a love of nature; in youth he developed passion for contemplation; and in full manhood he became at his time a leading exponent of the higher intellectual life, striving to propagate a taste in America for the then recently published works of Wordsworth and Coleridge. Dana's poetic study effected his own accomplishments in verse, which in their spiritual purpose were good, and in their descriptions of places familiar to him, were sincere and true. Dana died at Boston, February 2, 1879.

THE LITTLE BEACH-BIRD.

Thou little bird, thou dweller by the sea,
Why takest thou thy melancholy voice,
And with that boding cry
O'er the waves dost thou fly?
Oh ! rather, bird, with me
Through the fair land rejoice !

Thy flitting form comes ghostly dim and pale,
As driven by a beating storm at sea ;
Thy cry is weak and scared,
As if thy mates had shared
The doom of us.   Thy wail,—
What doth it bring to me ?

Thou call'st along the sand, and haunt'st the surge,
Restless and sad ; as if, in strange accord
With the motion and the roar
Of waves that drive to shore,
One spirit did ye urge—
The Mystery—the Word.

Of thousands, thou, both sepulchre and pall
Old ocean !   A requiem o'er the dead
From out thy gloomy cells
A tale of mourning tells,—
Tells of man's woe and fall,
His sinless glory fled.

Then turn thee, little bird, and take thy flight
Where the complaining sea shall sadness bring
Thy spirit never more.
Come, quit with me, the shore
For gladness and the light
Where birds of summer sing.

FITZ-GREENE HALLECK.

Fitz-Greene Halleck was one of the most famous poets of his day. He was born at Guilford, Conn., July 8, 1790. His education and his business vocation were not favorable to his development as a poet; and his inspiration seems rather to have been secondary than original, being imparted by personal contact with his friend Drake or by the reading of foreign poets, such as Burns and Campbell. Bryant, whose criticism of his intimates was sometimes less sure than friendly, has praised Halleck highly, but he is hardly read now. A few of his poems, however, such as *Burns*, are full of fine, manly passages; and of his nobility as a man his memorial exists in the reminiscences and in the biographies of him by his friends.

BURNS.[1]

Wild rose of Alloway,[2] my thanks ;
Thou 'mindst me of that autumn noon

[1] *Robert Burns*, a celebrated Scotch poet, born near the town of Ayr, in 1759.
[2] *Alloway Kirk*, the scene of Burns's *Tam o' Shanter*, is situated near the poet's birthplace.

When first we met upon " the banks
    And braes[1] o' bonny Doon."[2]

Like thine, beneath the thorn-tree's bough,
    My sunny hour was glad and brief,
We 've crossed the winter sea, and thou
    Art withered—flower and leaf.

And wilt not thy death-doom be mine—
    The doom of all things wrought of clay—
And withered my life's leaf like thine,
    Wild rose of Alloway ?

Not so his memory, for whose sake
    My bosom bore thee far and long,
His—who a humbler flower could make
    Immortal as his song.

The memory of Burns—a name
    That calls, when brimmed her festal cup,
A nation's glory in her shame,
    In silent sadness up.

A nation's glory—be the rest
    Forgot—she's canonized his mind ;
And it is joy to speak the best
    We may of human kind.

I 've stood beside the cottage-bed
    Where the Bard-peasant first drew breath ;
A straw-thatched roof above his head,
    A straw-wrought couch beneath.

---

[1] *Brae*, declivity or broken ground.
[2] *Doon*, a river not far from the birthplace of Burns, flowing into the Firth of Clyde.

And I have stood beside the pile,
   His monument—that tells to Heaven
The homage of earth's proudest isle
   To that Bard-peasant given !

Bid thy thoughts hover o'er that spot,
   Boy-minstrel, in thy dreaming hour ;
And know, however low his lot,
   A Poet's pride and power ;

The pride that lifted Burns from earth,
   The power that gave a child of song
Ascendancy o'er rank and birth,
   The rich, the brave, the strong ;

And if despondency weigh down
   Thy spirit's fluttering pinions, then
Despair—thy name is written on
   The roll of common men.

There have been loftier themes than his,
   And longer scrolls, and louder lyres,
And lays lit up with Poesy's
   Purer and holier fires.

Yet read the names that know not death ;
   Few nobler ones than Burns' are there ;
And few have won a greener wreath
   Than that which binds his hair.

His is that language of the heart,
   In which the answering heart would speak,
Thought, word, that bids the warm tear start,
   Or the smile light the cheek ;

And his that music, to whose tone
  The common pulse of man keeps time,
In cot or castle's mirth or moan,
  In cold or sunny clime.

And who hath heard his song, nor knelt
  Before its spell with willing knee,
And listened, and believed, and felt
  The Poet's mastery.

O'er the mind's sea, in calm and storm,
  O'er the heart's sunshine and its showers,
O'er Passion's moments bright and warm,
  O'er Reason's dark, cold hours ;

On fields where brave men " die or do,"
  In halls where rings the banquet's mirth,
Where mourners weep, where lovers woo,
  From throne to cottage-hearth ?

What sweet tears dim the eye unshed,
  What wild vows falter on the tongue,
When " Scots wha hae wi Wallace bled,"
  Or " Auld Lang Syne " is sung !

Pure hopes that lift the soul above,
  Come with his Cotter's hymn of praise,
And dreams of youth, and truth, and love,
  With " Logan's " [1] banks and braes.

And when he breathes his master-lay
  Of Alloway's witch-haunted wall,

[1] *Logan Water*, a rivulet in the parish of Kirkpatrick, Fleming,
Scotland, celebrated in modern and ancient Scottish song.

All passions in our frames of clay
  Come thronging at his call.

Imagination's world of air,
  And our own world, its gloom and glee,
With pathos, poetry, are there,
  And death's sublimity.

And Burns, though brief the race he ran,
  Though rough and dark the path he trod,
Lived—died—in form and soul a Man,
  The image of his God.

Through care, and pain, and want, and woe,
  With wounds that only death could heal,
Tortures—the poor alone can know,
  The proud alone can feel ;

He kept his honesty and truth,
  His independent tongue and pen,
And moved, in manhood as in youth,
  Pride of his fellow men.

Strong sense, deep feeling, passions strong,
  A hate of tyrant and of knave,
A love of right, a scorn of wrong,
  Of coward and of slave ;

A kind, true heart, a spirit high,
  That could not fear and would not bow,
Were written in his manly eye
  And on his manly brow.

Praise to the bard ! his words are driven,
  Like flower-seeds by the far winds sown,

Where'er, beneath the sky of heaven,
  The birds of fame have flown.

Praise to the man ! a nation stood
  Beside his coffin with wet eyes,
Her brave, her beautiful, her good,
  As when a loved one dies.

And still as on his funeral-day,
  Men stand his cold earth-couch around,
With the mute homage that we pay
  To consecrated ground.

And consecrated ground it is,
  The last, the hallowed home of one
Who lives upon all memories,
  Though with the buried gone.

Such graves as his are pilgrim-shrines,
  Shrines to no code or creed confined—
The Delphian [1] vales, the Palestines,
  The Meccas of the mind.

Sages, with wisdom's garland wreathed,
  Crowned kings, and mitred priests of power,
And warriors with their bright swords sheathed,
  The mightiest of the hour ;

And lowlier names, whose humble home
  Is lit by fortune's dimmer star,
Are there—o'er wave and mountain come,
  From countries near and far ;

[1] *Delphi*, the ancient oracle of Apollo, at the foot of Mount Parnassus in Greece.

Pilgrims whose wandering feet have pressed
   The Switzer's snow, the Arab's sand,
Or trod the piled leaves of the West,
   My own green forest-land.

All ask the cottage of his birth,
   Gaze on the scenes he loved and sung,
And gather feelings not of earth
   His fields and streams among.

They linger by the Doon's low trees,
   And pastoral Nith,[1] and wooded Ayr,[2]
And round thy sepulchres, Dumfries![3]
   The Poet's tomb is there.

But what to them the sculptor's art,
   His funeral columns, wreaths, and urns?
Wear they not graven on the heart
   The name of Robert Burns?

[1] *Nith*, a river flowing from Ayr into Solway Firth, eight miles south of Dumfries.

[2] *Ayr*, see note on *Burns*.

[3] *Dumfries*. Burns lived here during the latter part of his life, and his remains were transferred hither.

JOSEPH RODMAN DRAKE.

The life of Joseph Rodman Drake was cut short at the age of twenty-five. He showed, however, an early ability in the creation of fanciful poetry that gave him a place among the writers of his time. Drake was born in New York City, August 17, 1795. His first important literary undertaking was the part he took in the "Croaker" papers, but more interesting now, however, are his *American Flag* and *The Culprit Fay*. Drake died in New York, September 21, 1820.

THE AMERICAN FLAG.

When Freedom from her mountain height
Unfurled her standard to the air,
She tore the azure robe of night,
And set the stars of glory there.
She mingled with its gorgeous dyes
The milky baldric of the skies,
And striped its pure celestial white
With streakings of the morning light ;
Then from his mansion in the sun
She called her eagle bearer down,

And gave into his mighty hand
The symbol of her chosen land.

Majestic monarch of the cloud,
Who rear'st aloft thy regal form,
To hear the tempest trumpings loud
And see the lightning lances driven,
When strive the warriors of the storm,
And rolls the thunder-drum of heaven,
Child of the sun ! to thee 't is given
To guard the banner of the free,
To hover in the sulphur smoke,
To ward away the battle stroke,
And bid its blendings shine afar,
Like rainbows on the cloud of war,
The harbingers of victory !

Flag of the brave ! thy folds shall fly,
The sign of hope and triumph high,
When speaks the signal trumpet tone,
And the long line comes gleaming on.
Ere yet the life-blood warm and wet,
Has dimmed the glistening bayonet,
Each soldier eye shall brightly turn
To where thy sky-born glories burn,
And, as his springing steps advance,
Catch war and vengeance from the glance.
And when the cannon-mouthings loud
Heave in wild wreaths the battle-shroud,
And gory sabres rise and fall
Like shoots of flame on midnight's pall,
Then shall thy meteor glances glow,
And cowering foes shall sink beneath

Each gallant arm that strikes below
That lovely messenger of death.

Flag of the seas ! on ocean wave
Thy stars shall glitter o'er the brave ;
When death, careering on the gale,
Sweeps darkly round the bellied sail,
And frighted waves rush wildly back
Before the broadside's reeling rack,
Each dying wanderer of the sea
Shall look at once to heaven and thee,
And smile to see thy splendors fly
In triumph o'er his closing eye.

Flag of the free heart's hope and home !
By angel hands to valor given ;
Thy stars have lit the welkin dome,
And all thy hues were born in heaven.
Forever float that standard sheet !
Where breathes the foe but falls before us,
With Freedom's soil beneath our feet,
And Freedom's banner streaming o'er us?

JAMES GATES PERCIVAL.

James Gates Percival was a man of uncommon miscellaneous acquirements. He had an aptitude and a fluency for writing verse, but he suffered his facility to run unfettered so that his poetry had a tendency to wordiness and superficiality. Occasionally, however, in the description of quiet, beautiful scenes of simple nature, his success is commensurate with his attempt. Percival was born at Berlin, Conn., September 17, 1795, and died at Hazel Green, Wis., May 2, 1856.

TO A BUTTERFLY.

Thou, who in the early spring
Hoverest on filmy wing,
Visiting the bright-eyed flowers,
Fluttering in loaded bowers,
Settling on the reddening rose,
Reddening ere it fully blows,
When its crisp and folded leaves
   Just unroll their dewy tips,
   Soft as infant beauty's lips,
Or anything that love believes—

Little Wanderer after pleasure,
Where is that enchanted treasure
All that live are seeking for?
Is it in the blossom, or
Where we seek it, in the roses
  Of a maiden's cheek, or rather
  In the many lights that gather
When her smiling lip uncloses?
Wouldst thou rather kiss a flower,
When 't is dropping with a shower,
Or with trembling, quivering wing,
Rest thee on a dearer thing,
On a lip that has no stain,
On a brow that feels no pain,
In the beamings of an eye,
Where a world of visions lie,
Such as to the blest are given,
All of heaven—all of heaven?
If thou lovest the blossom, I
Love the cheek, the lip and eye.

GEORGE POPE MORRIS.

Morris was pre-eminently a writer of song. He was born at Philadelphia, October 10, 1802, and died at New York, July 6, 1864. Morris is strong in the expression of simple sentiments, such as are assured of the ready sympathy of the people. Of his poems, *Woodman, Spare that Tree!* is the best known; of others, his *Song of Marion's Men* is meritorious as a stirring and native ballad. These two poems and a few others will live with the songs of the nation, while his more ambitious efforts are already forgotten.

WOODMAN, SPARE THAT TREE!

Woodman, spare that tree !
  Touch not a single bough !
In youth it sheltered me,
  And I 'll protect it now.
'T was my forefather's hand
  That placed it near his cot ;
There, woodman, let it stand,
  Thy axe shall harm it not.

That old, familiar tree,
  Whose glory and renown
Are spread o'er land and sea—
  And would'st thou hew it down ?
Woodman, forbear thy stroke,
  Cut not its earth-bound ties ;
Oh, spare that aged oak,
  Now towering to the skies !

When but an idle boy,
  I sought its grateful shade ;
In all their gushing joy
  Here, too, my sisters played,
My mother kissed me here ;
  My father pressed my hand—
Forgive this foolish tear,
  But let that old oak stand !

My heart-strings round thee cling,
  Close as thy bark, old friend ;
Here shall the wild-bird sing,
  And still thy branches bend.
Old tree ! the storm still brave !
  And, woodman, leave the spot ;
While I 've a hand to save,
  Thy axe shall harm it not.

NATHANIEL PARKER WILLIS.

Nathaniel Parker Willis was a voluminous author, half dilettante, half in earnest, who held a leading position in his day in the literary society of New York. Willis was born at Portland, Maine, January 20, 1806. He was graduated at Yale, travelled abroad, edited journals in New York, and published volumes of light prose under such titles as *Sketches*, *Pencillings*, *Inklings*, *Loiterings*, etc. He was for a number of years associated with his friend Morris in editing the *Home Journal* of New York. His taste is lighter than that of most of his contemporaries of equal attainment, but for an idle hour his books are still pleasant reading, and have a value as pictures of the society of the time. The selection here given belongs to his more serious vein. Willis died January 20, 1867, at his cottage on the Hudson, near Newburgh, from which many of his sketches had been dated.

IDLENESS.

"Idleness sweet and sacred."
— *Walter Savage Landor.*[1]

"When you have found a day to be idle, be idle for a
    day.
When you have met with three cups to drink, drink your
    three cups."

The rain is playing its soft, pleasant tune
Fitfully on the skylight, and the shade
Of the fast flying clouds across my book
Passes with gliding change. My merry fire
Sings cheerfully to itself, my musing cat
Purrs as she wakes from her unquiet sleep,
And looks into my face as if she felt
Like me, the gentle influence of the rain.
Here I have sat since morn, reading sometimes,
And sometimes listening to the faster fall
Of the large drops, or rising with the stir
Of an unbidden thought, have walked awhile,
With the slow steps of indolence, my room,
And then sat down composedly again
To my quaint book of olden poetry.

It is a kind of idleness, I know ;
And I am said to be an idle man—
And it is very true, I love to go
Out in the pleasant sun, and let my eye
Rest on the human faces that pass by,
Each with its gay or busy interest :

[1] *Walter Savage Landor*, an eminent English author, born at
Ipsley Court, Warwickshire, in 1775.

And then I muse upon their lot, and read
Many a lesson in their changeful cast,
And so grow kind of heart, as if the sight
Of human beings bred humanity.
And I am better after it, and go
More grateful to my rest, and feel a love
Stirring my heart to every living thing;
And my low prayer has more humility;
And I sink lightlier to my dreams—and this,
'T is very true, is only idleness.

I love to go and mingle with the young
In the gay festal room—where every heart
Is beating faster than the merry tune,
And their blue eyes are restless, and their lips
Parted with eager joy, and their round cheeks
Flushed with the beautiful motion of the dance.
And I can look upon such things, and go
Back to my solitude, and dream bright dreams
For their fast coming years, and speak of them
Earnestly in my prayer, till I am glad
With a benevolent joy—and this, I know,
To the world's eye is only idleness.
And when the clouds pass suddenly away,
And the blue sky is like a newer world,
And the sweet growing things—forest and flower,
Humble and beautiful alike—are all
Breathing up odors to the very heaven—
Or when the frost has yielded to the sun
In the rich autumn, and the filmy mist
Lies like a silver lining on the sky,
And the clear air exhilarates, and life
Simply is luxury—and when the hush
Of twilight, like a gentle sleep, steals on,

And the birds settle to their nests, and stars
Spring in the upper sky, and there is not
A sound that is not low and musical—
At all these pleasant seasons, I go out
With my first impulse guiding me, and take
Wood-path or stream, or slope by hill or vale,
And in my recklessness of heart stray on,
Glad with the birds and silent with the leaves,
And happy with the fair and blessed world—
And this, 't is true, is only idleness !

And I should like to go up to the sky,
And course the heavens, like stars, and float away
Upon the gliding clouds that have no stay.
In their swift journey—and 't would be a joy
To walk the chambers of the deeps and tread
The pearls of its untrodden floor, and know
The tribes of the unfathomable depths—
Dwellers beneath the pressure of a sea !
And I should love to issue with the wind
On a strong errand, and o'er-sweep the earth
With its broad continents and islands green,
Like to the passing of a spirit on !
And this, 't is true, were only idleness.

CHARLES FENNO HOFFMAN.

During his earlier working years, Hoffman was one of the leading magazine writers of New York, and a facile writer of verse in various styles. He was born at New York in 1806. He studied at Columbia College and was admitted to the bar, but soon gave up the law for a literary career which he continued until the loss of his mind caused his permanent retirement to an asylum. He died at Harrisburg, Pennsylvania, June 7, 1884.

Under a mask of conventionality, Hoffman's verse reveals the nature of the man, buoyant, convivial, emotional, enthusiastic. This vivacity, however, is at times so gay as to seem to prophesy his sad end. Yet there were other things in Hoffman than mere lightness of spirit. He could work and work disinterestedly in a public cause; and the poem *Monterey* shows strength as well as a flashing intrepidity of spirit.

MONTEREY.

We were not many—we who stood
  Before the iron sleet that day ;
Yet many a gallant spirit would

Give half his years if he then could
    Have with us been at Monterey.

Now here, now there, the shot, it hailed
    In deadly drifts of fiery spray,
Yet not a single soldier quailed
When wounded comrades round them wailed
    Their dying shout at Monterey.

And on—still on our column kept
    Through walls of flames its withering way ;
Where fell the dead, the living stept,
Still charging on the guns which swept
    The slippery streets of Monterey.

The foe himself recoiled aghast,
    When striking where the strongest lay,
We swooped his flanking batteries past,
And braving full their murderous blast,
    Stormed home the towers of Monterey.

Our banners on those turrets wave,
    And there our evening bugles play ;
Where orange boughs above their grave
Keep green the memory of the brave
    Who fought and fell at Monterey.

We are not many—we who press'd
    Beside the brave who fell that day ;
But who of us has not confessed
He 'd rather share their warrior rest,
    Than not have been at Monterey?

ALBERT PIKE.

Albert Pike attempted much; he succeeded sometimes. Pike was born at Boston, Massachusetts, December 29, 1809. He entered Harvard, left for want of means, taught, travelled, edited, was a soldier, and after a long life died April 2, 1891.

Pike's best known poem is *Dixie*. Among the rest, perhaps the best in execution is *Every Year*. Pike's heartiness made his southern song a favorite even among veteran Union soldiers. *Every Year* has much of the same style of unselfishness and zeal. There is something noble, pure, and glorious about his lines that makes them of ideal value.

EVERY YEAR.

Life is a count of losses,
 Every year;
For the weak are heavier crosses
 Every year;
Lost Springs with sobs replying
Unto weary Autumn's sighing,
While those we love are dying,
 Every year.

The days have less of gladness
 Every year ;
The nights more weight of sadness
 Every year ;
Fair Springs no longer charm us,
The winds and weather harm us,
The threats of death alarm us,
 Every year.

There come new cares and sorrows
 Every year ;
Dark days and darker morrows,
 Every year ;
The ghosts of dead loves haunt us,
The ghosts of changed friends taunt us,
And disappointments daunt us,
 Every year.

To the past go more dead faces
 Every year,
As the loved leave vacant places,
 Every year ;
Everywhere the sad eyes meet us,
In the evening's dusk they greet us,
And to come to them entreat us,
 Every year.

"You are growing old," they tell us,
 Every year ;
"You are more alone," they tell us,
 Every year ;
"You can win no new affection,
You have only recollection,

Deeper sorrow and dejection,
    Every year."

Too true !   Life's shores are shifting
    Every year ;
And we are seaward drifting
    Every year ;
Old places, changing, fret us,
The living more forget us,
There are fewer to regret us,
    Every year.

But the truer life draws nigher
    Every year ;
And its morning-star climbs higher,
    Every year ;
Earth's hold on us grows slighter,
And the heavy burthen lighter,
And the Dawn Immortal brighter,
    Every year.

FRANCES SARGENT OSGOOD.

Frances Sargent Osgood was the first woman to write good poetry in this country. She was born at Boston, Massachusetts, June 18, 1811. She wrote poetry young, married, lived in England for several years, and returned to New England. She died at Hingham, Massachusetts, May 12, 1850. Several collections of her poems were published. She is especially successful with short poems of a character ardent, arch, and dreamy, such as *A Dancing Girl*, *Calumny*, and *He may go—if he can*.

THE DANCING GIRL.

She comes—the spirit of the dance !
    And, but for those large, eloquent eyes,
Where passion speaks in every glance,
    She 'd seem a wanderer from the skies.

So light, that gazing breathless there,
    Lest the celestial dream should go,
You 'd think the music in the air
    Waved the fair vision to and fro !

Or that the melody's sweet flow
   Within the radiant creature played,
And those soft wreathing arms of snow
   And white sylph feet the music made.

Now gliding slow with dreamy grace,
   Her eyes beneath their lashes lost,
Now motionless with lifted face,
   And small hands on her bosom crossed ;

And now with flashing eyes she springs—
   Her whole bright figure raised in air,
As if her soul had spread its wings
   And poised her one wild instant there !

She spoke not ; but so richly fraught
   With language was her glance and smile,
That when the curtain fell, I thought
   She had been talking all the while.

WILLIAM ROSS WALLACE.

William Ross Wallace was born at Lexington, Ky., in 1819. He practiced law in New York after 1841, and contributed occasionally for magazines. He died at New York, May 5, 1881. Wallace had the sense of literary patriotism and the gift of rhetoric, rather than natural poetic inspiration. His poems, however, are in their way praiseworthy. Among them, *Of Thine Own Country Sing* is characterized by its breadth and vigor of treatment, by the clear and well-proportioned presentation of his theme. This piece recalls some of the shorter poems of Coleridge.

OF THINE OWN COUNTRY SING.

I met the wild-eyed Genius of our land
    In Huron's forest vast and dim ;
I saw her sweep a harp with stately hand ;
    I heard her solemn hymn.

She sang of nations that had passed away
    From her own broad imperial clime ;
Of nations new to whom she gave the sway :
    She sang of God and Time.

I saw the Past with all its rhythmic lore ;
  I saw the Present clearly glow ;
Shapes with pale faces paced a far dim shore
  And whispered " Joy " and "Woe ! "

Her large verse pictured mountain, vale, and bay ;
  Our wide, calm rivers rolled along,
And many a mighty lake and prairie lay
  In the shadow of her song.

As in Missouri's mountain range, the vast
  Wild wind majestically flies
From crag to crag, till on the top at last
  The wild wind proudly dies.

So died the hymn, " O, Genius ! how can I
  Crown me with song as thou art crowned ? "
She, smiling, pointed to the spotless sky
  And the forest-tops around,—

Then sang—" Not to the far-off lands of Eld
  Must thou for inspiration go ;
There Milton's large imperial organ swelled,
  There Avon's [1] waters flow.

" No alien-bard, where Tasso's [2] troubled lyre
  Made sorrow fair, unchallenged dwells—
Where deep-eyed Dante [3] with the wreath of fire
  Came chanting from his hells.

---

[1] *Avon*, a river of England which flows by Shakespeare's birth-place, Stratford.

[2] *Tasso*, an Italian poet, b. at Sorrento, in 1544.

[3] *Dante Alighieri*, author of *Divine Comedy*, one of the greatest poets who ever lived, b. at Florence, Italy, in 1265.

" Yet sometimes sing the old majestic themes
 Of Europe in her song enshrined :
These, going wind-like o'er the Sea of Dreams,
 May liberalize the mind.

" Or learn from mournful Asia, as she lies
 Musing at noon beneath her stately palms,
Her angel-lore, her wide-browed prophecies,
 Her solemn-sounding psalms.

"Or sit with Afric [1] when her eyes of flame
 Smoulder in dreams, beneath their swarthy lids,
Of youthful Sphinx, and kings at loud acclaim
 On new-built pyramids.

"But know thy Highest dwells at Home : there art
 And choral inspiration spring ;
If thou wouldst touch the universal heart,
 Of thine own country sing."

[1] *Afric.* Africa.

JOHN GODFREY SAXE.

John Godfrey Saxe is a genius by himself. Saxe
was born at Highgate, Vt., June 2, 1816. He was
graduated at Middlebury College, entered the bar,
edited a newspaper, and held political offices. He
also wrote for magazines and published several volumes of poetry. A leading quality of much of his
verse is humor. On sober subjects, for instance in
Murillo and his Slave, he has also done good work.
The verses by Saxe excel by virtue of plain, honest
statement, and are even sometimes wanting in literary finish. Saxe died at Albany, N. Y., March 31,
1887.

MURILLO AND HIS SLAVE.

A LEGEND OF SPAIN.

" Whose work is this ? " Murillo said,
   The while he bent his eager gaze
Upon a sketch (a Virgin's head)
   That filled the painter with amaze.

Of all his pupils, not a few,—
    Marvelling, 't would seem no less than he ;
Each answered that he nothing knew
    As touching whose the sketch might be.

This much appeared, and nothing more :
    The piece was painted in the night :
" And yet, by Jove ! " Murillo swore,
    " He has no cause to fear the light."

" ' T is something crude, and lacks, I own,
    That finer finish time will teach ;
But genius here is plainly shown,
    And art beyond the common reach.

" Sebastian ! " (turning to his slave,)
    " Who keeps this room when I 'm in bed ? "
" ' T is I, Señor."   " Now mark you, knave !
    Keep better watch," the master said ;

" For if this painter comes again,
    And you, while dozing, let him slip,
Excuses will be all in vain,—
    Remember, you shall feel the whip ! "

Now while Sebastian slept, he dreamed
    That to his dazzled vision came
The Blessed Lady—so she seemed—
    And crowned him with a wreath of Fame.

Whereat the startled slave awoke,
    And at his picture wrought away
So rapt that ere the spell was broke,
    The dark was fading into day.

"My beautiful!" the artist cried;
  "Thank God, I have not lived in vain!"
Hark! 'T is Murillo at his side;
  The man has grown a slave again.

"Who is your master?—answer me!"
  "'T is you," replied the faltering lad.
"Nay, 't is not that, I mean," said he,
  "Tell me, what teacher have you had?"

"Yourself, Señor.   When you have taught
  These gentlemen, I too have heard
The daily lesson, and have sought
  To treasure every golden word."

"What say you, boys?"   Murillo cried.
  Smiling in sign of fond regard,
"Is this a case—pray you decide—
  For punishment, or for reward?"

"Reward, Señor!" they all exclaimed,
  And each proposed some costly toy;
But still, whatever gift was named,
  Sebastian showed no gleam of joy.

Whereat one said: "He's kind to-day;
  Ask him your Freedom."   With a groan
The boy fell on his knees: "Nay, nay!
  My father's freedom, not my own."

"Take both!" the painter.   "Henceforth
  A slave no more,—be thou my son;
Thy Art had failed, with all its worth,
  Of what thy Heart this day has won!"

L'ENVOI.

The traveller, loitering in Seville,
   And gazing at each pictured saint,
May see Murillo's genius still,
   And learn how well his son could paint.

HENRY DAVID THOREAU.

Thoreau was an eccentric recluse, who, in his own way, however, had found out many reasons why life is worth living. Henry David Thoreau was born at Concord, Massachusetts, July 12, 1817. He was graduated at Harvard, built him a hut on the edge of Walden Pond, near his native town, and lived for a number of years without the aid of human society. He spent much of his time out of doors in the observation of nature, occupying himself also in the study of the great authors of the past. Thoreau was well versed in the lore of wild nature. He was also an original thinker on certain literary and ethical subjects in which he found himself specially interested. He was distinctively a poet in his imagination and fancy, and in his power of imbuing himself with the spirit of the woods in which he lived, but his more important literary productions, such as *Walden, A Week on the Concord and Merrimac*, etc., took the form of prose. *The Fishing Boy* is an example of what he could do in verse with a subject which appealed to his personal sympathies.

THE FISHING BOY.

My life is like a stroll upon the beach,
    As near the ocean's edge as I can go ;
My tardy steps its waves sometimes o'er-reach
    Sometimes I stay to let them overflow.

My sole employment is, and scrupulous care,
    To place my gains beyond the reach of tides,
Each smoother pebble, and each shell more rare,
    Which ocean kindly to my hand confides.

I have but few companions on the shore :
    They scorn the strand who sail upon the sea ;
Yet oft I think the ocean they 've sailed o'er
    Is deeper known upon the strand to me.

The middle sea contains no crimson dulse,[1]
    Its deeper waves cast up no pearls to view ;
Along the shore my hand is on its pulse,
    And I converse with many a ship-wrecked crew.

And since in life I loved them well,
    Let me in death lie down with them,
And let the pines and tempests swell
    Around me their great requiem.

[1] *Dulse*, a kind of seaweed.

THOMAS BUCHANAN READ.

Thomas Buchanan Read, whose ambition it was to be an artist, is now better remembered by his poems. Read was born in Chester County, Pennsylvania, March 12, 1822. He studied, first in the large cities of this country, then in the galleries of Florence and Rome. Read died in New York, May 11, 1872. In Read's poetry, which contains traces of his artistic sense, he has excelled in several different styles. *Sheridan's Ride* is famous; *Drifting* and *The Closing Scene* are hardly less so. Others are almost as good: *The Song of the Alpine Guide*, *The Closing Scene*, or the sonnet *I Have Looked on a Face*, should all be read in order to fill out that idea of Read's capability which is only partly revealed through the two former.

SONG OF THE ALPINE GUIDE.

On Zurich's [1] spires, with rosy light,
  The mountains smile at morn and eve,
And Zurich's waters, blue and bright,
  The glories of those hills receive.

[1] *Zurich*, a beautiful city of Switzerland.

And there my sister trims her sail,
    That like a wayward swallow flies ;
But I would rather meet the gale,
    That fans the eagle in the skies.

She sings in Zurich's chapel choir,
    Where rolls the organ on the air,
And bells proclaim from spire to spire
    Their universal call to prayer.
But let me hear the mountain rills,
    And old Saint Bernard's[1] storm-bell toll,
And, 'mid these great cathedral hills,
    The thundering avalanches roll.

My brother wears a martial plume,
    And serves within a distant land,—
The flowers that on his bosom bloom
    Are placed there by a stranger hand.
Love greets him but in foreign eyes,
    And greets him in a foreign speech,
But she who to my heart replies
    Must speak the tongue these mountains teach.

The warrior's trumpet o'er him swells,
    The triumph which it only hath ;
But let me hear the mule-worn bells
    Speak peace in every mountain heath.
His spear is ever 'gainst a foe,
    Where waves the hostile flag abroad ;
My pike-staff only clears the snow,
    My banner the blue sky of God.

---

[1] *Saint Bernard*, the well-known hospice of Saint Bernard.

On Zurich's side my mother sits,
   And to her whirling spindle sings ;
Through Zurich's waves my father's nets
   Sweep daily with their filmy wings,
To that beloved voice I list ;
   And view that father's toil with pride ;
But like a low and vale-born mist,
   My spirit climbs the mountain side.

And I would ever hear the stir
   And turmoil of the singing winds,
Whose viewless wheels around me whirr,
   Whose distaffs are the swaying pines,
And on some snowy mountain's head,
   The deepest joy to me is given,
Where, net-like, the great storm is spread
   To sweep the azure lake of Heaven.

Then since the vale delights me not,
   And Zurich wooes in vain below,
And it hath been my joy and lot
   To scale these Alpine crags of snow—
And since in life I loved them well,
   Let me in death lie down with them,
And let the pines and tempests swell
   Around me their great requiem.

GUY HUMPHREYS McMASTER.

The poem, *The Old Continentals*, or, as it has also been aptly called, *Carmen Bellicosum*, should, as well as the name of the author, be kept from oblivion. Judge Guy Humphreys McMaster was born at Clyde, N. Y., January 31, 1829. He wrote the poem at nineteen years of age, and it appeared soon after in the *Knickerbocker Magazine* of February, 1849, over the signature " John MacGrom." The piece is the best extant imaginative description of the Revolutionary soldier, with his quaint garb covering a grim determination. McMaster died at Bath, N. Y., in September, 1887.[1]

CARMEN BELLICOSUM.

In their ragged regimentals,
Stood the old Continentals,
    Yielding not,
When the Grenadiers were lunging,
And like hail fell the plunging

[1] I am indebted for these facts to a notice in the *New York Critic*, vol. viii., p. 203 (erroneously given vol. xi., in *Poole's Index*), including extracts from a letter by Mr. E. C. Stedman.

Cannon-shot ;
When the files
Of the isles,
From the smoky night encampment,
Bore the banner of the rampant
Unicorn,
And grummer, grummer, grummer,
Rolled the roll of the drummer
Through the morn !

Then with eyes to the front all,
And with guns horizontal,
Stood our sires ;
And the balls whistled deadly,
And in streams flashing redly
Blazed the fires ;
As the roar
On the shore,
Swept the strong battle-breakers o'er the green-sodded
acres
Of the plain :
And louder, louder, louder,
Cracked the black gunpowder,
Cracking amain !

Now like smiths at their forges
Worked the red St. George's
Cannoniers,
And the " villainous saltpetre "
Rang a fierce discordant metre
Round their ears ;
As the swift
Storm-drift,

With hot sweeping anger, came the horse-guards' clangor
  On our flanks.
  Then higher, higher, higher burned
  The old-fashioned fire
   Through the ranks !

  Then the old-fashioned colonel
  Galloped through the white infernal
   Powder-cloud ;
  And his broad sword was swinging,
  And his brazen throat was ringing,
   Trumpet-loud.
   Then the blue
   Bullets flew,
And the trooper-jackets redden at the touch of the
   leaden
   Rifle-breath.
And rounder, rounder, rounder, roared the iron six-
   pounder,
   Hurling death.

JOHN ANTROBUS.

One American poem has been written by an artist not a native of this country. John Antrobus, the author of *The Cow-boy*, was born at Walsall, Staffordshire, England, in 1831, but came to America at the age of eighteen. He gained some repute as a painter, and has also published other poetry than the present selection. *The Cow-boy* is a vivid picture, especially successful in the half-careless, half-artful refrain at the close of each stanza.

THE COW-BOY.

"What care I, what cares he,
What cares the world of the life we know !
Little they reck of the shadowless plains,
The shelterless mesa, the sun and the rains,
The wild, free life, as the winds that blow."
  With his broad sombrero,[1]
  His worn chapparejos,
  And clinking spurs,

[1] *Sombrero*, a kind of broad-brimmed hat.

Like a Centaur he speeds,
Where the wild bull feeds ;
And he laughs ha, ha ! who cares, who cares !

Ruddy and brown—careless and free—
A king in the saddle—he rides at will
O'er the measureless range where rarely change
The swart gray plains so weird and strange,
Treeless, and streamless, and wondrous still !
　　With his slouch sombrero,
　　His torn chapparejos,
　　And clinking spurs
　　Like a Centaur he speeds
　　Where the wild bull feeds :
And he laughs ha, ha ! who cares, who cares !

He of the towns, he of the East,
Has only a vague, dull thought of him ;
In his far-off dreams the cow-boy seems
A mythical thing, a thing he deems
A Hun or a Goth, as swart and grim !
　　With his stained sombrero,
　　His rough chapparejos,
　　And clinking spurs,
　　Like a Centaur he speeds
　　Where the wild bull feeds ;
And he laughs ha, ha ! who cares, who cares !

Often alone, his saddle a throne,
He scans like a sheik the numberless herd ;
Where the buffalo-grass and the sage-grass dry
In the hot white glare of a cloudless sky,
And the music of streams is never heard.
　　With his gay sombrero,

His brown chapparejos,
And clinking spurs,
Like a Centaur he speeds,
Where the wild bull feeds ;
And he laughs ha, ha ! who cares, who cares !

Swift and strong, and ever alert,
Yet sometimes he rests on the dreary vast ;
And his thoughts, like the thoughts of other men,
Go back to his childhood's days again,
And to many a loved one in the past.
    With his gay sombrero,
    His rude chapparejos,
    And clinking spurs,
    He rests awhile,
    With a tear and a smile,
Then he laughs ha, ha ! who cares, who cares !

Sometimes his mood from solitude
Hurries him heedless off to the town !
Where mirth and wine through the goblet shine,
And treacherous sirens twist and twine
The lasso that often brings him down ;
    With his soaked sombrero,
    His rent chapparejos,
    And clinking spurs,
    He staggers back
    On the homeward track,
And shouts to the plains—who cares, who cares !

'T is over late at the ranchman's gate—
He and his fellows, perhaps a score,
Halt in a quarrel o'er night begun,
With a ready blow and a random gun—

There 's a dead, dead comrade ! nothing more.
With his slouched sombrero,
His dark chapparejos,
And clinking spurs,
He dashes past,
With face o'ercast,
And growls in his throat—who cares, who cares !

Away on the range there is little change ;
He blinks in the sun, he herds the steers ;
But a trail on the wind keeps close behind,
And whispers that stagger and blanch the mind
Through the hum of the solemn noon he hears ;
With his dark sombrero,
His stained chapparejos,
And clinking spurs,
He sidles down.
Where the grasses brown
May hide his face, while he sobs—who cares !

But what care I, and what cares he—
This is the strain, common at least ;
He is free and vain of his bridle-rein,
Of his spurs, of his gun, of the dull, gray plain ;
He is ever vain of his broncho' beast !
With his gray sombrero,
His brown chapparejos,
And clinking spurs,
Like a Centaur he speeds,
Where the wild bull feeds ;
And he laughs, ha, ha !—who cares, who cares !

¹ *Broncho*, a horse not broken ; a western word.

11. At Swords' Points.

THE war songs of 1861–65 struck a new chord on the national harp. Never before in this country had battle been urged by poetry so good in itself; and never before had American literature shown such fire in its notes of feeling.[1]

The bards of one side replying, as it were, to those of the other, the ballads have an antiphonal interest. The southern lyrics are parts of the past; but as truly national to us, as the Celtic odes are to England; echoes lovely in their life and their picturesqueness, and attractive from their sentiment of fellowship and their hatred of fancied tyranny. The northern poems are sterner, deeper, and more serious; less adventurous, it is true, but fully as determined in their strenuous resolution for victory. They are also inclined less to self-glorification and more toward unselfish passion for the preservation of the Union. On both sides, though there are certain minstrels distinguished by a stronger and a more frequent touch than the others, the interest of the war ballads of '61 is rather national than personal.

General reference: American War Ballads. G. P. Putnam's Sons.

[1] In response to the request of my publishers, I am glad to be able to append here Holmes's *Old Ironsides*, a poem on a war-ship, and thus related psychologically to this group.

JULIA WARD HOWE.

Julia Ward Howe was born in New York, May 27, 1819.

> " She with all the charm of woman,
> She with all the breadth of man,"

as seen in her writings, has been distinguished rather as a reformer on the lecture platform and with the pen, than as a poet. In the *The Battle-Hymn of the Republic*, however, her nature comes out at its strongest, under manifestations seen only partially and occasionally in her other poems.

BATTLE-HYMN OF THE REPUBLIC.

Mine eyes have seen the glory of the coming of the Lord :
He is trampling out the vintage where the grapes of wrath
    are stored ;
He hath loosed the fateful lightning of his terrible swift
    sword :
       His truth is marching on.

I have seen Him in the watch-fires of a hundred circling
      camps ;
They have builded Him an altar in the evening dews and
      damps ;
I can read His righteous sentence by the dim and flaring
      lamps :
        His day is marching on.

I have read a fiery gospel writ in burnish'd rows of steel :
" As ye deal with my condemners, so with you my grace
      shall deal ;
Let the Hero, born of woman, crush the serpent with his
      heel,
        Since God is marching on."

He has sounded forth the trumpet that shall never call
      retreat ;
He is sifting out the hearts of men before His judgment-
      seat ;
Oh, be swift, my soul, to answer Him ! be jubilant, my
      feet !
        Our God is marching on.

In the beauty of the lilies Christ was born across the sea,
With a glory in His bosom that transfigures you and me :
As He died to make men holy, let us die to make men
      free,
        While God is marching on.

November, 1861.

JAMES THOMAS FIELDS.

James Thomas Fields, genial publisher, man of letters, and literary enthusiast, was born at Portsmouth, N. H., December 31, 1816. He had intimate and friendly relations with the leading poets, not merely as their man of business, but also as the companion of their social hours. Lowell has dedicated one of his volumes to Fields, and Whittier has left a pen portrait of him in his *Tent on the Beach*. As a writer of verse, Fields's hearty energetic character comes out in the poem, *The Stars and Stripes*. Fields died at Boston, Mass., April 24, 1881.

THE STARS AND STRIPES.

Rally round the flag, boys—
Give it to the breeze !
That 's the banner we bore
On the land and seas.

Brave hearts are under it,
Let the *traitors* brag,
Gallant lads, fire away !
And fight for the flag.

Fields.

Their flag is but a rag—
    Ours is the true one;
Up with the Stars and Stripes!
    Down with the new one!

Let our colors fly, boys—
    Guard them day and night;
For victory is liberty,
    And God will bless the right.

ALBERT PIKE.

(For biographical notice see the poem, *Every Year*.)

DIXIE. [1]

Southrons, hear your country call you!
Up, lest worse than death befall you!
To arms! To arms! To arms, in Dixie!
  Lo! all the beacon-fires are lighted—
  Let all hearts be now united!
To arms! To arms! To arms, in Dixie!
    Advance the flag of Dixie!
    Hurrah! Hurrah!
    For Dixie's land we take our stand,
    And live or die for Dixie!
    To arms! To arms!
    And conquer peace for Dixie!

[1] Dixie was the name given by the Southerners to the territory of the eleven Confederate States which seceded in 1861. It is derived from the old Mason and Dixon's line, which under one of the several Congressional compromises, had been fixed to divide slave territory from free.

I quote from a letter in my possession from Mr. Yvon Pike, who writes:

"My father wrote two poems entitled *Dixie*, one in 1861, and the other [which I have not seen] just after the war."

To arms ! To arms !
And conquer peace for Dixie !

Hear the Northern thunders mutter !
Northern flags in South winds flutter !
　　　To arms !
Send them back your fierce defiance !
Stamp upon the accursed alliance !
　　　To arms !
　　Advance the flag of Dixie !

Fear no danger ! shun no labor !
Lift up rifle, pike, and sabre !
　　　To arms !
Shoulder pressing close to shoulder,
Let the odds make each heart bolder !
　　　To arms !
　　Advance the flag of Dixie !

How the South's great heart rejoices
At your cannon's ringing voices !
　　　To arms !
For faith betrayed, and pledges broken,
Wrongs inflicted, insults spoken,
　　　To arms !
　　Advance the flag of Dixie !

Strong as lions, swift as eagles,
Back to their kennels hunt these beagles !
　　　To arms !
Cut the unequal bond asunder !
Let them hence each other plunder !
　　　To arms !
　　Advance the flag of Dixie !
13

Swear upon your country's altar
Never to submit or falter !
   To arms !
Till the spoilers are defeated,
Till the Lord's work is completed,
   To arms !
  Advance the flag of Dixie !

Halt not till our Federation
Secures among earth's powers its station !
   To arms !
Then at peace, and crowned with glory,
Hear your children tell the story !
   To arms !
  Advance the flag of Dixie !

If the loved ones weep in sadness,
Victory soon shall bring them gladness.
   To arms !
Exultant pride soon banish sorrow ;
Smiles chase tears away to-morrow.
To arms ! To arms ! To arms, in Dixie !
   Advance the flag of Dixie !
   Hurrah ! hurrah !
   For Dixie's land we take our stand,
   And live or die for Dixie !
   To arms ! To arms !
   And conquer peace for Dixie !
   To arms ! To arms !
And conquer peace for Dixie !

ROSSITER WORTHINGTON RAYMOND.

Rossiter Worthington Raymond was born at Cincinnati, Ohio, April 27, 1840. He is known rather as a scientist than as a man of letters, but among other writings he has composed several war-ballads. Of these his *Cavalry Song* is the best.

CAVALRY SONG.

Our bugles sound gayly. To horse and away !
And over the mountains breaks the day ;
Then ho ! brothers, ho ! for the ride or the fight,
There are deeds to be done ere we slumber to-night !
    And whether we fight or whether we fall
    By sabre-stroke or rifle ball,
    The hearts of the free will remember us yet,
    And our country, our country will never forget !

Then mount and away ! let the coward delight
To be lazy all day and safe all night ;
Our joy is a charger, flecked with foam,
And the earth is our bed and the saddle our home ;
    And whether we fight, etc.

See yonder the ranks of the traitorous foe,
And bright in the sunshine bayonets glow !
Breathe a prayer, but no sigh ; think for what you would
    fight ;
Then charge ! with a will boys, and God for the right !
    And whether we fight, etc.

We have gathered again the red laurels of war ;
We have followed the traitors fast and far ;
But some who rose gayly this morn with the sun
Lie bleeding and pale on the field they have won !
    But whether we fight, etc.

JAMES RYDER RANDALL.

James Ryder Randall was born at Baltimore, Md., January 1, 1829. He studied at Georgetown College, and later removed to Louisiana. Since then he has held several editorial positions in the South.

Randall was one of the leading poets of the Lost Cause. His production was prolific; his style is fresh, spirited, and chivalric. *My Maryland* is his best lyric. *There 's Life in the Old Land Yet* has in it very quotable lines. Among others of excellence are *John Pelham*, and the poem beginning, "Weep, Louisiana, weep." Randall's fault, if it be one in a war song—vituperation—is more than atoned for by his energy and vividness.

MY MARYLAND.

The despot's heel is on thy shore,
   Maryland !
His torch is at thy temple door,
   Maryland !
Avenge the patriotic gore

That flecked the streets of Baltimore,[1]
And be the battle queen of yore,
    Maryland, my Maryland !

Hark to an exiled son's appeal,
    Maryland !
My Mother State, to thee I kneel,
    Maryland !
For life or death, for woe or weal,
Thy peerless chivalry reveal,
And gird thy beauteous limbs with steel,
    Maryland, my Maryland !

Thou wilt not cower in the dust,
    Maryland !
Thy beaming sword shall never rust,
    Maryland !
Remember Carroll's [2] sacred trust,
Remember Howard's [3] warlike thrust,
And all thy slumberers with the just,
    Maryland, my Maryland !

Come ! 't is the red dawn of the day,
    Maryland !
Come with thy panoplied array,
    Maryland !

[1] *Baltimore*, referring to the conflict of the Sixth Massachusetts Regiment with the people of Baltimore, on passing through the town.

[2] *Charles Carroll, of Carrollton*, Revolutionary patriot, born at Annapolis, in 1737,

[3] *John Eager Howard*, a distinguished military officer, born in Baltimore Co., Md., in 1752.

With Ringgold's [1] spirit for the fray,
With Watson's [2] blood at Monterey,
With fearless Lowe [2] and dashing May,[2]
    Maryland, my Maryland !

Dear Mother, burst the tyrant's chain,
    Maryland !
Virginia should not call in vain,
    Maryland !
She meets her sisters on the plain,
" *Sic semper !* " 't is the proud refrain
That baffles minions back amain,
    Maryland !
Arise in majesty again,
    Maryland, my Maryland !

Come ! for thy shield is bright and strong.
    Maryland !
Come ! for thy dalliance does thee wrong,
    Maryland !
Come to thine own heroic throng
Stalking with liberty along,
And chant thy dauntless slogan-song,[3]
    Maryland, my Maryland !

I see the blush upon thy cheek,
    Maryland !
But thou wast ever bravely meek,
    Maryland !

[1] *Major Samuel Ringgold*, born in Washington Co., Md., in 1800.
[2] *Watson ; Lowe ; May ;* Maryland soldiers of local fame.
[3] *Slogan Song*, war cry ; used first of a Highland clan in Scotland.

But lo ! there surges forth a shriek,
From hill to hill, from creek to creek,
Potomac calls to Chesapeake,
    Maryland, my Maryland !

Thou wilt not yield the Vandal toll,
    Maryland !
Thou wilt not crook to his control,
    Maryland !
Better the fire upon thee roll,
Better the shot, the blade, the bowl,
Than crucifixion of the soul,
    Maryland, my Maryland !

I hear the distant thunder hum
    Maryland !
The " Old Line's " bugle, fife, and drum,
    Maryland !
She is not dead, nor deaf, nor dumb ;
Huzza ! she spurns the Northern scum—
She breathes ! she burns ! She 'll come ! She 'll
    come !
    Maryland, my Maryland !

EDMUND CLARENCE STEDMAN.

Edmund Clarence Stedman was born at Hartford, Conn., October 8, 1833. He studied at Yale College, and in his varied career has been editor, critic, essayist, stock-broker, and last but not least, poet. Stedman's largest literary work of general interest is his *Poets of America*, but his *Victorian Poets* has won fame for its thorough knowledge of the subject, and for its keen yet temperate criticism. Of his own poems, those which deal with war subjects have won the largest measure of appreciation, and, by their force of unconscious sincerity and passion, are considered to surpass their author's more ornate poems on classical subjects. *Wanted—A Man* is the chief among these war ballads; others that ought to be mentioned are *Sumter* and *Treason's Last Device*. An exquisite fancy, one of the most charming productions of American verse, which does not belong to the war ballads, is the *Pan in Wall Street*.

WANTED—A MAN.[1]

Back from the trebly crimsoned field
　　Terrible words are thunder-tost ;
Full of the wrath that will not yield,
　　Full of revenge for battles lost !
Hark to their echo, as it crost
　　The Capital, making faces wan :
End this murderous holocaust ;
　　Abraham Lincoln, give us a MAN !

Give us a man of God's own mould,
　　Born to marshal his fellow-men ;
One whose fame is not bought and sold
　　At the stroke of a politician's pen ;
Give us the man of thousands ten,
　　Fit to do as well as to plan ;
Give us a rallying cry, and then,
　　Abraham Lincoln, give us a MAN ?

No leader to shirk the boasting foe,
　　And to march and countermarch our brave,
Till they fall like ghosts in the marshes low,
　　And swamp-grass covers each nameless grave ;
Nor another, whose fatal banners wave
　　Aye in disaster's shameful van ;
Nor another, to bluster, and lie, and rave,—
　　Abraham Lincoln, give us a MAN !

---

[1] This virile cry for a fit leader for the Army of the Potomac was inspired by an editorial article of Henry J. Raymond in the *New York Times*. It was written in 1862, when the popular feeling of chagrin and humiliation over McClellan's failure and Pope's disaster at Manassas was most intense. Mr. Lincoln was so strongly impressed by the poem that he read it to his Cabinet.

Hearts are mourning in the North,
  While the sister rivers seek the main,
Red with our life-blood flowing forth—
Who shall gather it up again?
Though we march to the battle-plain
  Firmly as when the strife began,
Shall all our offering be in vain?—
  Abraham Lincoln, give us a MAN!

Is there never one in all the land,
  One on whose might the Cause may lean?
Are all the common ones so grand,
  And all the titled ones so mean!
What if your failure may have been
  In trying to make good bread from bran,
From worthless metal a weapon keen?—
  Abraham Lincoln, find us a MAN!

Oh, we will follow him to the death,
Where the foeman's fiercest columns are!
Oh, we will use our latest breath,
  Cheering for every sacred star!
His to marshal us high and far;
  Ours to battle, as patriots can
When a hero leads the Holy War!—
  Abraham Lincoln, give us a MAN!

JAMES SLOAN GIBBONS.

James Sloan Gibbons was born at Wilmington, Delaware, July 1, 1820. The song here quoted was published in 1862, but was until lately printed anonymously. The poem, with its splendid single line refrain, was Gibbons's only noted purely literary work ; but he was as zealous in behalf of anti-slavery as might be expected from the tone of his verses. His house in New York was sacked in the anti-slavery riots of 1863. Gibbons died at New York City, October 17, 1892.

THREE HUNDRED THOUSAND MORE.

We are coming, Father Abraham, three hundred thousand
  more,
From Mississippi's winding stream and from New Eng-
  land's shore ;
We leave our ploughs and workshops, our wives and
  children dear,
With hearts too full for utterance, with but a silent tear ;
We dare not look behind us, but steadfastly before :
We are coming, Father Abraham, three hundred thousand
  more !

If you look across the hill-tops that meet the northern sky,
Long moving lines of rising dust your vision may descry ;
And now the wind, an instant, tears the cloudy veil aside,
And floats aloft our spangled flag in glory and in pride.
And bayonets in the sunlight gleam, and bands brave
    music pour ;
We are coming, Father Abraham, three hundred thousand
    more !

If you look all up our valleys where the growing harvests
    shine,
You may see our sturdy farmer boys fast forming into
    line ;
And children from their mother's knees are pulling at
    the weeds,
And learning how to reap and sow against their country's
    needs ;
And a farewell group stands weeping at every cottage
    door :
We are coming, Father Abraham, three hundred thousand
    more !

You have called us and we 're coming, by Richmond's
    bloody tide,
To lay us down for Freedom's sake, our brothers' bones
    beside,
Or from foul treason's savage grasp to wrench the mur-
    derous blade,
And in the face of foreign foes its fragments to parade.
Six hundred thousand loyal men and true have gone
    before :
We are coming, Father Abraham, three hundred thousand
    more !

GEORGE HENRY BOKER.

George Henry Boker was born at Philadelphia,
Penn., October 6, 1823, and died there January 2,
1890. Boker is the American who perhaps has most
fully possessed the dramatic faculty. His best known
play is *Francesca da Rimini*. Boker excels in the
delineation of strenuous, often uncontrolled passion,
both in long scenes and in short lyrics. Paolo, in the
dialogue with Francesca is perhaps too improbably
analytical in his reflections, which in its parts is also
unequal in merit. But in this drama and in the
poem, *The Varuna*, which in its progress perhaps
slackens a little in movement, owing to imperfect
narration, there is still powerful work.

THE VARUNA.

Who has not heard of the dauntless *Varuna?*
  Who has not heard of the deeds she has done?
Who shall not hear, while the brown Mississippi
  Rushes along from the snow to the sun?

Crippled and leaking she entered the battle,
  Sinking and burning she fought through the fray;

Crushed were her sides and the waves ran across her,
　Ere, like a death-wounded lion at bay,
Sternly she closed in the last fatal grapple,
　Then in her triumph moved grandly away.

Five of the rebels, like satellites round her,
　Burned in her orbit of splendor and fear ;
One, like the pleiad of mystical story,
　Shot, terror-stricken, beyond her dread sphere.

We who are waiting with crowns for the victors,
　Though we should offer the wealth of our stores,
Load the *Varuna* from deck down to kelson,
　Still would be niggard, such tribute to pour
On courage so boundless.　It beggars possession,—
　It knocks for just payment at Heaven's bright door !

Cherish the heroes who fought the *Varuna* ;
　Treat them as kings if they honor your way ;
Succor and comfort the sick and the wounded ;
　Oh ! for the dead let us all kneel to pray !

NATHANIEL GRAHAM SHEPHERD.

Nathaniel Graham Shepherd was born at New York, in 1835. He was a journalist, and at the time of the civil war a war correspondent. Among several war-poems which he has written, *Roll Call* is the most popular. Shepherd died at New York, May 23, 1869.

ROLL-CALL.

"Corporal Green!" the Orderly cried;
　"Here!" was the answer, loud and clear,
　From the lips of the soldier who stood near,—
And "Here!" was the word the next replied.

"Cyrus Drew!"—then a silence fell;
　This time no answer followed the call;
　Only his rear-man had seen him fall;
Killed or wounded—he could not tell.

There they stood in the failing light,
　These men of battle, with grave, dark looks,
　As plain to be read as open books,
While slowly gathered the shades of night.

The fern on the hill-sides was splashed with blood,
  And down in the corn where the poppies grew
  Were redder stains than the poppies knew ;
And crimson-dyed was the river's flood.

For the foe had crossed from the other side
  That day, in the face of a murderous fire
  That swept them down in its terrible ire,
And their life-blood went to color the tide.

"Herbert Kline !"   At the call there came
  Two stalwart soldiers into the line,
  Bearing between them this Herbert Kline,
Wounded and bleeding, to answer his name.

" Ezra Kerr ! "—and a voice answered, " Here ! "
  " Hiram Kerr ! "—but no man replied.
  They were brothers, these two ; the sad winds sighed,
And a shudder crept through the cornfield near.

" Ephraim Deane ! "—then a soldier spoke ;
  " Deane carried our regiment's colors," he said ;
  " Where our ensign was shot I left him dead,
Just after the enemy wavered and broke.

" Close to the roadside his body lies ;
  I paused a moment and gave him a drink ;
  He murmured his mother's name, I think,
And death came with it, and closed his eyes."

'T was a victory ; yes, but it cost us dear,—
  For that company's roll, when called at night,
  Of a hundred men who went into the fight,
Numbered but twenty that answered " Here ! "

ABRAHAM JOSEPH RYAN.

Abraham Joseph Ryan was born at Norfolk, Va., August 15, 1839. Father Ryan was a Catholic priest, and a confederate chaplain through the war. He was also a writer of war-poems, known most widely by *The Conquered Banner*, in which with the old fervor for that flag which

"will live in song and story,"

is mingled decisive resignation and counsel to

"Furl that Banner, softly, slowly!"—

and to

"Let it droop there, furled forever,—
For its people's hopes are fled."

Ryan died at Louisville, Ky., April 22, 1886.

THE CONQUERED BANNER.

Furl that Banner, for 't is weary,
Round its staff 't is drooping dreary;
    Furl it, fold it,—it is best;
For there 's not a man to wave it,

And there 's not a sword to save it,
And there 's not one left to lave it
In the blood which heroes gave it,
And its foes now scorn and brave it ;
    Furl it, hide it,—let it rest !

Take that Banner down ! 't is tattered ;
Broken is its staff and shattered,
And the valiant hosts are scattered
    Over whom it floated high ;
Oh, 't is hard for us to fold it,
Hard to think there 's none to hold it,
Hard that those who once unrolled it
    Now must furl it with a sigh !

Furl that Banner—furl it sadly ;
Once ten thousands hailed it gladly,
And ten thousands wildly, madly,
    Swore it should forever wave—
Swore that foemen's swords could never
Hearts like theirs entwined dissever,
And that flag should wave forever
    O'er their freedom, or their grave !

Furl it !—for the hands that grasped it,
And the hearts that fondly clasped it,
    Cold and dead are lying low ;
And the Banner—it is trailing,
While around it sounds the wailing,
    Of its people in their woe ;
For though conquered, they adore it—
Love the cold dead hands that bore it,
Weep for those who fell before it,

Pardon those who trailed and tore it ;
And, oh, wildly they deplore it,
  Now to furl and fold it so !

Furl that Banner !   True 't is gory,
Yet 't is wreathed around with glory,
And 't will live in song and story
  Though its folds are in the dust !
For its fame on brightest pages,
Penned by poets and by sages,
Shall go sounding down the ages—
  Furl its folds though now we must !

Furl that Banner, softly, slowly ;
Treat it gently—it is holy,
  For it droops above the dead ;
Touch it not—unfold it never ;
Let it droop there, furled forever,—
  For its people's hopes are fled.

OLIVER WENDELL HOLMES.

(For biographical notice see under "Classics.")

OLD IRONSIDES.

Ay, tear her tattered ensign down !
  Long has it waved on high,
And many an eye has danced to see
  That banner in the sky ;
Beneath it rung the battle shout,
  And burst the cannon's roar ;—
The meteor of the ocean air
  Shall sweep the clouds no more.

Her deck, once red with heroes' blood,
  Where knelt the vanquished foe,
When winds were hurrying o'er the flood,
  And waves were white below,
No more shall feel the victor's tread,
  Or know the conquered knee ;
The harpies of the shore shall pluck
  The eagle of the sea !

O better that her shattered hulk
  Should sink beneath the wave;
Her thunders shook the mighty deep,
  And there should be her grave;
Nail to the mast her holy flag,
  Set every thread-bare sail,
And give her to the god of storms,
  The lightning and the gale!

III. Contemporaries.

THE war-ballads of 1861, and the poems of authors for the most part still living, form the characteristic element in the verse of the country for the last forty years. What shall be said of it? Has it continued the poetic tradition formed by the "Classics?" And what has been its own force and indication?

Considering the general dearth of poetry throughout the civilized world as compared to the splendid lyric flowering of half or three quarters of a century ago, it is not strange that America does not at this moment teem with new and stirring poetry. On the other hand, the total amount of the poetry current has been greater than might be estimated from the common reference and the rather general disparagement. By careful comparison and collation of dates, it could be readily shown that the last twenty-five years has been one of the most fruitful periods for poetry in America, perhaps only second in value to the twenty-five years, of which 1850 was the centre.[1] This productiveness has not been confined to those

[1] Reckon up, for instance, what Lowell has written since the *Commemoration Ode*, Whittier since *The Tent on the Beach*, and all that Lanier has written; and add the poems of Miller, Bret Harte, O'Reilly, Riley, Woodberry, and others.

whose names have for nearly fifty years been historic. On the contrary, while few have startled with claims for greatness, poetry as an art has been widespread; more literary workmen than ever before have had skill and have secured for it recognition, and sincerity in the expression of the poet's personality has been greater than any imitative dependence on foreign models.

Another advance has been in the evolution of individuals or groups in different sections of the country, who have, in a measure, given the feeling and the physiognomy of their locality. New England had already been sung; but as an expression of the breadth of national life and consciousness, have appeared singers in New York, in the South, in the middle West, and in California. Others have presented their own emotions as dominant over the intellectual wealth of the Old World.

Among this poetry, the verse written in New York has possibly had the greatest breadth and national character; not only the scenes of the city itself, but those of the country as a whole, and often world-wide themes have attracted writers. The South has a poetry of peace as well as of war which may be characterized as being proudly and loyally self-centred. The middle West has been the least fertile of all. We do not know that region yet in its capacity for suggestiveness. Noteworthy, however, is the Californian group, whose productions have shown luxuriant fancy, but have been somewhat stinted by lack of favorable material conditions in their section of the country. With reference to the whole group of

"Contemporaries," it may be noted that there has been a good deal of attention to form. Slovenliness has been a less common fault than artificiality; and while a studied disregard of art has made its appearance once, it has not found favor. Perhaps, however, too much attention has been paid to form, and too little to matter. For form itself is only a means to an end, although, on the lower plane of subjects, it sometimes deceives by seeming to be an end in itself; and in successful higher work by being almost identical with its idea. Whitman, Taylor, and Lanier are in this period figures all worthy of special study, and the selections from them have therefore been put in a subdivision by themselves. Other poets have written work which in a general consideration cannot be overlooked. Of them, the most picturesque and striking figure has been Joaquin Miller. He is a poet by temperament, but one of a temperament more common in the early years of the century than in these days of colder blood. His poems have a wealth and gorgeousness of color that no American has equalled. Of late his work has exhibited signs of a revising care that not all poets give. Thomas Bailey Aldrich is a poet of exquisite culture. John Boyle O'Reilly had a life and character more worthy even than the metrical frame which surrounds the sketch of it. Among the poets of the South, Hayne possessed a gentleness and humor, and Timrod a thought and seriousness that render them both of marked attractiveness.

Without mentioning others, it may be said that for few in this period has poetry been constantly the one aim. With some it is only an utterance of momentary youthful sentiment; others have not reached any real mastery until after middle life. For most of them, apparently, nature and experience are not rich enough, or perseverance in the poetic direction great enough, for filling out a life devoted to the Muses.

For the few, however, who would have devoted themselves thus, those to whom health or wealth or life itself were as nothing in their eyes in comparison with the prize of their high calling, circumstances have been hard, though never wholly baffling. No one of these men has, like Lanier, died so young as to fail in entering on the path of glory; though no one of them has as yet achieved the assured fame of a " classic."

Some one has said that the present ideal in American poetry is an aggregation of distinct types. For the successful master of the verse of his land the ideal is rather an assimilation of these types by the artist, a reconstruction and reproportioning to a fairer whole.

Such a purpose is not, perhaps, out of reach of the lyrist; but there are some signs of movement toward drama, which is better adapted to the vast and varied phenomena of a nation's life. Thus far, attempts have been few, and if popular, they have been rude in form and primitive in treatment; but the drama which is both representative and civilized must show both the plainest and the stateliest of life, subject to such dramatic conditions as come into existence only at rare epochs.

CHRISTOPHER PEARSE CRANCH.

Christopher Pearse Cranch was born at Alexandria, Va., March 8, 1813. He was a painter and a poet, residing in Europe for several years, later on Staten Island, in Cambridge, and in New York. Cranch died at Cambridge, Mass., January 20, 1892.

Cranch's poetry is a union of the grave and the gay. One might, on the reading of some pieces of his, ascribe to him a perpetual and irrepressible liveliness, were it not for his lines of sober meditation. An instance of this latter style is found in the *Stanzas*, which flow forth, however, with as graceful limpidity as any of his lighter productions.

STANZAS.

Thought is deeper than all speech
   Feeling deeper than all thought
Souls to souls can never teach
   What unto themselves was taught.

We are spirits clad in veils :
   Man by man was never seen ;

All our deep communion fails
  To remove the shadowy screen.

Heart to heart was never known ;
  Mind with mind did never meet ;
We are columns left alone,
  Of a temple once complete.

Like the stars that gem the sky,
  Far apart, though seeming near,
In our light we scattered lie ;
  All is thus but starlight here.

What is social company
  But a babbling summer stream ?
What our wise philosophy
  But the glancing of a dream ?

Only when the sun of love
  Melts the scattered stars of thought ;
Only when we live above
  What the dim-eyed world hath taught ;

Only when our souls are fed
  By the font which gave them birth,
And by inspiration led,
  Which they never drew from earth,

We, like parted drops of rain
  Swelling till they meet and run,
Shall be all absorbed again,
  Melting, flowing into one.

WILLIAM WETMORE STORY.

William Wetmore Story, represents at present more completely than any other, the American artist at once in marble and in song. Story was born at Salem, Mass., February 12, 1819, and is the son of Chief Justice Story. He was graduated at Harvard and entered the bar, but settled in Italy in 1848. Besides his sculpture, he has given to the world volumes of poems in his youth and age. His subjects deal with the region of the purely cultivated tastes rather than with the every-day life of the people.

THE THREE SINGERS.

"Where is a singer to cheer me ?
My heart is weary with sadness,
I long for a verse of gladness !"
Thus cried the Shah to his Vizier.

He sat on his couch of crimson,
And silent he smoked, and waited,
Till a youth with face elated,
Entered, and bent before him.

He swung the harp from his shoulder,
And ran o'er its strings, preluding,
O'er his thought for a moment brooding,
Then his song went up into sunshine.

It leaped like the fountain, breaking
At the top of its aspiration,
It fell from its culmination,
In tears, to life's troubled level.

He sang of the boundless future,
That had the gates of the morning,
His fancies the song adorning,
Like pearls on a white-necked maiden.

" My hope, like a hungered lion,"
He sang, " for its prey is panting ;
Oh ! what is so glad, so enchanting
As Manhood, and Fame, and Freedom.

"To youth there is nothing given,
The fruit on the high palm groweth,
And thither life's caravan goeth,
For rest and delight in its shadow."

He ceased,—and the Shah, half smiling,
Beckoned, and said, " Stay near me,
Your song hath a charm to cheer me :
Ask ! what you ask shall be given.

" Now bring me that other singer,
That ere I was born, enchanted
The world with a song undaunted ! "
They went,—and an old man entered.

His forehead beneath his turban
Was wrinkled,—he entered slowly,—
Bending—and bending more lowly,
Waited,—the Shah commanded—

" Sing me a song ; " his fingers
Over the light strings trembled,
And the sounds of the strings resembled
The wind, in the cypresses grieving.

He sang of the time departed,
In his song, as in some calm river,
Where temples and palm-trees quiver,
But pass not—his youth was imaged.

" Our shadow that lay behind us,
Ere the noon-day sun passed o'er us,
Now darkens the path before us,
As we walk away from our morning.

" Oh ! where are the friends that beside us,
Walked in the garden of roses ;
The dear head no longer reposes
On the bosom, to feel the heart's beating.

" Oh, Life ! 't is a verse so crooked,
On Fate's sharp scimitar written,
And Joy—a pomegranate bitten
By a worm that preys at its centre."

He ceased, and the harp's vibration
Throbbed only,—a slow tear twinkled
On the rim of those eyes, so wrinkled,
And the fountain renewed its plashing.

The Shah was silent—a dimness
Clouded his eyes—from his finger
He drew a great ruby—the singer
Bowed low at this token of honor.

At last, from his musing arousing,
He spoke, " Is there none you can bring me
The praise of the present to sing me.
Seek him and bring him before me."

He waited—the morning—the noonday
Passed—at last, when the shadows
Lengthened on gardens and meadows,
A poor, maimed cripple, they brought him.

"What ! *you* sing the praise of the present ;
You, by Fortune and Fate so forsaken,
What charms can the Present awaken ?"
" I love and am loved," was the answer.

THOMAS WILLIAM PARSONS.

Thomas William Parsons is best known as the author of the lines *On a Bust of Dante*. He was born at Boston, Mass., August 18, 1819. He gave himself thoroughly to the study of Italian, especially Dante, spending much time in Italy. Parsons died at Scituate, Mass., September 3, 1892.

The themes of his poems are usually of a grave and elevated order. A number of them have a stern, tragic beauty, which is largely subjective with their artist.

ON A BUST OF DANTE.

See, from this counterfeit of him
    Whom Arno [1] shall remember long,
How stern of lineament, how grim,
    The father was of Tuscan song !
There but the burning sense of wrong,
    Perpetual care and scorn, abide ;
Small friendship for the lordly throng ;
    Distrust of all the world beside.

[1] *Arno*, An Italian river flowing through Florence.

Faithful if this wan image be,
  No dream his life was,—but a fight !
Could any Beatrice see
  A lover in that anchorite ?
To that cold Ghibeline's [1] gloomy sight
  Who could have guessed the visions came
Of Beauty, veiled with heavenly light,
  In circles of eternal flame ?

The lips as Cumæ's [2] cavern close,
  The cheeks with fast and sorrow thin.
The rigid front, almost morose,
  But for the patient hope within,
Declare a life whose course hath been
  Unsullied still, though still severe,
Which, through the wavering days of sin,
  Kept itself icy-chaste and clear.

Not wholly such his haggard look
  When wandering once, forlorn, he strayed,
With no companion save his book,
  To Corvo's hushed monastic shade ;
Where, as the Benedictine laid
  His palm upon the pilgrim guest,
The single boon for which he prayed
  Was peace, that pilgrim's one request.

Peace dwells not here—this rugged face
  Betrays no spirit of repose ;
The sullen warrior sole we trace,
  The marble man of many woes.

---

[1] *Ghibeline*, a political party in Florence.
[2] *Cumæ*, a preclassic town of Italy where dwelt the Sibyl.

Such was his mien when first arose
    The thought of that strange tale divine,
When hell he peopled with his foes,
    The scourge of many a guilty line.

War to the last he waged with all
    The tyrant canker-worms of earth ;
Baron and Duke, in hold and hall,
    Cursed the dark hour that gave him birth.
He used Rome's harlot for his mirth ;
    Plucked bare hypocrisy and crime,
But valiant souls of knightly worth
    Transmitted to the rolls of Time.

Oh Time ! whose verdicts mock our own,
    The only righteous judge art thou !
That poor, old exile, sad and lone,
    Is Latium's[1] other Virgil now :
Before his name the nations bow ;
    His words are parcel of mankind,
Deep in whose hearts, as on his brow,
    The marks have sunk of Dante's mind.

---

[1] *Latium*, the ancient name of the region of Italy whence arose the Latins.

ALICE CARY.

Alice Cary was born at Miami Valley, near Cincinnati, Ohio, April 20, 1820. While still young, she published, in collaboration with her sister Phœbe Cary, various single poems, and in 1850 her first volume. She died in New York, February 12, 1871.

Much of Alice Cary's work has the true poetic method of indirectness, especially in *The Gray Swan*. The details of this story are suggested rather than expressed; the gradual revealing of the sailor's identity, the emotions of the mother, and the character of the sailor are presented with art. In this respect the poem is one of the finest in American literature.

THE GRAY SWAN.

" Oh tell me, sailor, tell me true,
Is my little lad, my Elihu
A-sailing with your ship ? "
The sailor's eyes were dim with dew,—
" Your little lad, your Elihu ? "
He said with trembling lip,—
" What little lad ? what ship ? "

"What little lad! as if there could be
Another such an one as he!
What little lad, do you say?
Why, Elihu, that took to the sea
The moment I put him off my knee;
It was just the other day
The *Gray Swan* sailed away."

"The other day?" the sailor's eyes
Stood open with a great surprise,—
"The other day? the *Swan*?"
His heart began in his throat to rise.
"Ay, ay, sir, here in the cupboard lies
The jacket he had on."
"And so your lad is gone?"

"Gone with the *Swan*." "And did she stand
With her anchor clutching hold of the sand
For a month and never stir?"
"Why, to be sure! I've seen from the land,
Like a lover kissing his lady's hand,
The wild sea kissing her,—
A sight to remember, sir."

"But, my good mother, do you know
All this was twenty years ago?
I stood on the *Gray Swan's* deck,
And to that lad I saw you throw,
Taking it off, as it might be, so!
The kerchief from your neck."
"Ay, and he'll bring it back!"

"And did the little lawless lad
That has made you sick and made you sad,
Sail with the *Gray Swan's* crew?"

"Lawless ! the man is going mad !
The best boy ever mother had,—
Be sure he sailed with the crew !
What would you have him do ? "

" And he has never written line
Nor sent you word, nor made you sign
To say he was alive ? "
" Hold ! if 't was wrong, the wrong is mine ;
Besides, he may be in the brine ?
And could he write from the grave ?
Tut, man ? what would you have ? "

" Gone twenty years,—a long, long cruise,—
'T was wicked thus your love to abuse ;
But if the lad still live
And come back home, think you you can
Forgive him ? "   " Miserable man,
You 're mad as the sea,—you rave,—
What have I to forgive ? "

The sailor twitched his shirt so blue,
And from within his bosom drew
The kerchief.   She was wild.
" My God ! my Father ! is it true ?
My little lad, my Elihu !
My blessed boy, my child !
My dead, my living child ! "

THOMAS WENTWORTH HIGGINSON.

Thomas Wentworth Higginson was born at Cambridge, Mass., December 22, 1823. He was graduated at Harvard, became an ardent anti-slavery agitator, and had an honorable career in the war as an officer of colored troops. For much of his life he has given himself to literary pursuits. Besides essays and stories, he has published a series of poems, some of which are marked by exuberance of joyous emotion.

THE MADONNA DI SAN SISTO.[1]

Look down into my heart,
Thou holy mother, with thy holy Son !
Read all my thoughts and bid the doubts depart,
And all the fears be done.

I lay my spirit bare,
O blessed ones, beneath your wondrous eyes,
And not in vain ; ye hear my heart-felt prayer,
And your twin-gaze replies.

[1] *The Madonna di San Sisto*, Raphael's most celebrated Madonna.

What says it ? All that life
Demands of those who live, to be and do,—
Calmness in all its bitterest, deepest still ;
Courage, till all is through.

Thou mother ! in thy sight
Can aught of passion or despair remain ?
Beneath those eyes' serene and holy light
The soul is bright again.

Thou Son ! whose earnest gaze
Looks ever forward, fearless, steady, strong ;
Beneath those eyes no doubt or weakness stays,
Nor fear can linger long.

Thanks, that to my weak heart
Your mingled powers, fair forms, such counsel give,
Till I have learned the lesson ye impart,
I have not learned to live.

And oh, till life is done,
Of your deep gaze may ne'er the impression cease !
Still may the dark eyes whisper, "Courage ! On ! "
The mild eyes murmur, " Peace ! "

RICHARD HENRY STODDARD.

Richard Henry Stoddard has won fame as poet, critic, and man of letters, while bound for many years by the responsibilities of business or of office. Stoddard was born at Hingham, Mass., July 2, 1825. He has published a number of volumes of verse, of which the earliest bears date 1849. He has been an old associate and friend of Bayard Taylor and of Stedman.

Stoddard's verse takes a wide range. It would be impossible in a brief mention to touch upon all his poetic undertakings; but he is forcible alike in themes of home or of foreign lands. Stoddard's literary qualities are grace of fancy, strength, spontaneity, and sincerity.

THE COUNTRY LIFE.

Not what we would, but what we must,
Makes up the sum of living;
Heaven is both more and less than just
In taking and in giving.
Swords cleave to hands that sought the plough,
And laurels miss the soldier's brow.

Me, whom the city holds, whose feet
Have worn its stony highways,
Familiar with its loneliest street,—
Its ways were never my ways.
My cradle was beside the sea,
And there, I hope, my grave will be.

Old homestead !—in that old, gray town
Thy wave is seaward blowing ;
Thy slip of garden stretches down
To where the tide is flowing ;
Below they lie, their sails all furled,
The ships that go about the world.

Dearer that little country house,
Inland, with pines beside it ;
Some peach trees with unfruitful boughs,
A well, with weeds to hide it ;
No flowers, or only such as rise
Self-sown,—poor things !—which all despise.

Dear country home ! can I forget
The least of thy sweet trifles ?
The windows—vines that clamber yet,
Whose bloom the bee still rifles ?
The roadside blackberries, growing ripe,
And in the woods the Indian Pipe ?

Happy the man who tills his field,
Content with rustic labor ;
Earth does to him her fulness yield,
Hap what may to his neighbor.
Well days, sound nights,—oh, can there be
A life more rational and free ?

Dear country life of child and man !
For both the best and strongest,
That with the earliest race began,
And hast outlived the longest :
Their cities perished long ago,
Who the first farmers were we know.

Perhaps our Babels too will fall ;
If so, no lamentations,
For Mother Earth will shelter all,
And feed the unborn nations !
Yes, and the swords that menace now
Will then be beaten to the plough.

LUCY LARCOM.

Lucy Larcom was born at Beverly, Mass., in 1826. In her early life she associated closely with working people, and from this experience she has drawn much of the material in her songs of labor. Some of Lucy Larcom's work has homely qualities, and resembles certain of the poems of Whittier, with whom she has had an intimate literary friendship. Her verse has also picturesque elements, and the more ethereal thought which springs from brooding on the nature of flowers and of clouds. A spiritual touch is thus infused into her poetry, refining the most common subjects, and giving them the liveliness which, with a certain clear cut-purpose, constitutes the charm of her poems.

A HAREBELL.

Mother, if I were a flower,
Instead of a little child,
I would choose my home by a waterfall,
To laugh at its gambols wild,
To be sprinkled with spray and dew ;
And I 'd be a harebell blue.

Blue is the color of heaven,
And blue is the color for me.
But in the rough earth my clinging roots
Closely nestled should be ;
For the earth is friendly and true
To the little harebell blue.

I could not look up to the sun
As the bolder blossoms look ;
But he would look up with a smile to me
From his mirror in the brook ;
And his smile would thrill me through,
A trembling harebell blue.

The winds would not break my stem
When they rushed in tempest by ;
I would bend before them, for they come
From the loving Hand on high,
That never a harm can do
To a slender harebell blue.

I would play with shadow and breeze ;
I would blossom from June till frost.
Dear Mother, I know you would find me out,
When my stream-side cliff you crossed ;
And I 'd give myself to you—
Your own little harebell blue.

ROSE TERRY COOKE.

Rose Terry Cooke was born at West Hartford, Conn., February 17, 1827, and died at Pittsfield, Mass., July 18, 1892. Mrs. Cooke has published several volumes of poems. In some of her work, as in that of most women who write verse, emotion is somewhat too restless, and ambitions are too little subdued and guided. In certain of her pieces, however, of a modest effort, womanly feeling is gracefully presented. Mrs. Cooke's method is, under a light and fanciful guise, to advance true criticism of life. *Columbine* and *Indolence* are two of her best poems.

COLUMBINE.

Little dancing harlequin !
Thou thy scarlet bells dost ring
When the merry western wind
Gives their slender stems a swing ;
Every yellow butterfly,
Rising on the fragrant air ;
Glittering insects everywhere,
Moths that in the dead leaves lie,
List the tinkling chime that tells
Of the Spring's aërial spells.

In the long and shining days
May-time swings to mother Earth,
From the stony crevices
Dry with sun and grey with dearth,
Where no other bloom can cling,
Thou dost lift thy dainty spire,
Slight and subtle mist of fire
O'er the rock face shimmering,
Nodding, swaying, scattering wide
Flame and gold on every side.

No faint odor fills thy cup,
Nothing knowest thou but cheer,
Over thee no memory
Floats its pennant sad and dear.
Gay and fleeting as is laughter,
Or a little joyful song
Wandering the woods along,
That no echo cometh after ;
Idle moth and strenuous bee
Know that honey dwells in thee.

When thy motley opens wide,
Then the summer draweth near ;
Then the sunshine shall abide,
Vanished is the winter fear,
Snowdrifts never come again
When thou standest sentinel,
Shouting gayly : "All is well,"
To the blooms on hill and plain
Summer-bringing columbine,
Make thy happy errand mine.

THOMAS BAILEY ALDRICH.

Thomas Bailey Aldrich was born at Portsmouth, N. H., November 11, 1836. He was prevented, on account of the death of his father, from carrying out a purpose he had formed of going to college, and devoted himself instead, to writing for the press. At the age of twenty he published *The Ballad of Baby Bell*, which is as fresh now as when written, and may perhaps still be considered his best poem. *Wedded* shows his exquisite finish of style, and his power of fitly condensing strong emotion into a short poem. He has written some charming prose stories and studies, based on the New England life he knows so well.

WEDDED.

(Provençal Air.[1])

The happy bells shall ring,
Marguerite ;
The summer birds shall sing,
Marguerite—

[1] *Provençal*, the Romance language used in the south of France.

You smile, but you shall wear
Orange-blossoms in your hair,
    Marguerite.

Ah me ! the bells have rung,
    Marguerite ;
The summer birds have sung—
    Marguerite—
But cypress-leaf and rue
Make a sorry wreath for you,
    Marguerite.
16

ELIZABETH AKERS ALLEN.

Elizabeth Akers Allen was born at Strong, Franklin County, Maine, October 9, 1832. She published a volume of poetry in 1852, and a second in 1867. Since then her writings have received a large measure of popular appreciation. She is remarkable as a poet of the love that is irrespective of sex. Her best known poem is *Backward, Turn Backward, O Time, in Your Flight.* *The Grass Is Greener Where She Sleeps* is, however, simpler and less conventional in tone. Other poems of a like description are the sonnet, *A Dream*, and *A Spring Love-Song*.

THE GRASS IS GREENER WHERE SHE SLEEPS.

The grass is greener where she sleeps,
  The birds sing softlier there,
And nature fondliest vigil keeps
  Above a face so fair,—
For she was innocent and sweet
  As mortal thing can be,—

The only heart that ever beat
  That beat alone for me.
To me her dearest thoughts were told,
  Her sweetest carols sung ;
To her my love song never old,
  My face was always young.
Ah, life seems drear and little worth,
  Since she has ceased to be,—
The only heart in all the earth
  That never loved but me.

CELIA LAIGHTON THAXTER.

The poems of Celia Thaxter are such as no one could write who did not know by continuous observations the wonder and beauty of the sea.

Celia Laighton Thaxter was born at Portsmouth, N. H., in 1836. Her girlhood was spent on the Isles of Shoals, where her father was light-house keeper. She has published several volumes of poems, some of the most characteristic of which describe the more sombre features of the seashore, such as the ocean tempest, the emotions of the watchers on the land, and the shipwreck.

THE MINUTE-GUNS.

I stood within the little cove,
    Full of the morning's life and hope,
While heavily the eager waves
    Charged thundering up the rocky slope.

The splendid breakers! How they rushed
    All emerald green and flashing white,
Tumultuous in the morning sun,
    With cheer and sparkle and delight!

And freshly blew the fragrant wind,
　The wild sea-wind, across their tops,
And caught the spray and flung it far,
　In sweeping showers of glittering drops.

Within the cove all flashed and foamed
　With many a fleeting rainbow hue ;
Without, gleamed bright against the sky,
　A tender wavering line of blue,

Where tossed the distant waves, and far
　Shone silver white a quiet sail ;
And overhead the soaring gulls
　With graceful pinions stemmed the gale.

And all my pulses thrilled with joy,
　Watching the winds' and waters' strife,
With sudden rapture, and I cried,
　"Oh, sweet is life ! Thank God, for life !"

Sailed any cloud across the sky,
　Marring this glory of the sun's ?
Over the sea from distant forts,
　There came the boom of minute-guns !

War tidings !　Many a brave soul fled
　And many a heart the message stuns !
I saw no more the joyous waves,
　I only heard the minute-guns.

HENRY TIMROD.

Henry Timrod was born at Charleston, S. C., December 8, 1829. He studied at the University of Georgia, and afterwards tried journalism, but died after a rather sad experience of ill-health and poverty, at Columbia, S. C., October 6, 1867.

Timrod is a poet less known doubtless than he might well be. He has written several war songs which are excellent of their kind. His best piece of work, however, is *The Cotton Boll*, which combines description and reverie, and in which he has given evidence of capacity that his shortened life did not permit him fully to develop.

THE COTTON BOLL.[1]

While I recline
At ease beneath
This immemorial pine,
Small sphere !
(By dusky fingers brought this morning here
And shown with boastful smiles),

[1] The *boll* is the seed vessel of the cotton.

I turn thy cloven sheath,
Through which the soft white fibres peer,
That, with their gossamer bands,
Unite, like love, the sea-divided lands,
And slowly, thread by thread,
Draw forth the folded strands,
Than which the trembling line,
By whose frail help yon startled spider fled
Down the tall spear-grass from his swinging bed,
Is scarce more fine ;
And as the tangled skein
Unravels in my hands,
Betwixt me and the noon-daylight
A veil seems lifted, and for miles and miles
The landscape broadens on my sight,
As, in the little boll, there lurked a spell
Like that which, in the ocean shell,
With mystic sound,
Breaks down the narrow walls that hem us round,
And burns some city here
Into the restless main,
With all his capes and isles !

Yonder bird,
Which floats, as if at rest,
In those blue tracts above the thunder, where
No vapors cloud the stainless air,
And never sound is heard,
Unless at such rare time
When, from the City of the Blest,
Rings down some golden chime,
Sees not from his high place
So vast a cirque of summer space
As widens round me in one mighty field,

Which, rimmed by seas and sands,
Doth hail its earliest daylight in the beams
Of gray Atlantic dawns ;
And, broad as realms made up of many lands,
Is lost afar
Behind the crimson hill and purple lawns
Of sunset, among plains which roll their streams
Against the Evening Star !
And lo !
To the remotest point of sight
Although I gaze upon no waste of snow,
The endless field is white ;
And the whole landscape glows,
For many a shining league away,
With such accumulated light
As Polar lands would flash beneath a tropic day !
Nor lack there (for the vision grows,
And the small charm within my hands—
More potent even than the fabled one,
Which oped whatever golden mystery
Lay hid in fairy wood or magic vale,
The curious ointment of the Arabian tale—
Beyond all mortal sense
Doth stretch my sight's horizon, and I see,
Beneath its simple influence,
As if, with Uriel's [1] crown,
I stood in some great temple of the Sun.
And looked, as Uriel down !)
Nor lack here pastures rich and fields all green

[1] *Uriel,* " God's Light," the archangel,
  " One of the seven
  Who in God's presence, nearest to his throne,
  Stand ready at command."
  MILTON, *Paradise Lost.*

With all the common gifts of God.
For temperate airs and torrid sheen
Weave Edens of the sod ;
Through lands which look one sea of billowy gold
Broad rivers wind their devious ways ;
A hundred aisles in their embraces fold
A hundred luminous bays ;
And through yon purple haze
Vast mountains lift their plumèd peaks, cloud crowned ;
And, save where up their sides the ploughman creeps,
An unhewn forest girds them grandly round,
In whose dark shades a future navy sleeps !
Ye Stars, which, though unseen, yet with me gaze
Upon this loveliest fragment of the earth !
Thou Sun, that kindlest all thy gentlest rays
Above it, as to light a favorite hearth !
Ye Clouds, that in your temples in the West
See nothing brighter than the humblest flowers !
And you, ye Winds, that on the ocean's breast
Are kissed to coolness ere ye reach its bowers !
Bear witness with me in my song of praise,
And tell the world that, since the world began,
No fairer land hath fired a poet's lays,
Or given a home to man.

But these are charms already widely blown !
His be the meed whose pencil's trace
Hath touched our very swamps with grace,
And round whose tuneful way
All Southern laurels bloom ;
The Poet of " The Woodlands " unto whom
Alike are known
The flute's low breathing and the trumpet's tone,
And the soft west wind's sighs ;

But who shall utter all the debt,
O Land wherein all powers are met
That bind a people's heart,
The world doth owe thee at this day,
And which it never can repay,
Yet scarcely deigns to own !
Where sleeps the poet who shall fitly sing
The source wherefrom doth spring
That mighty commerce which, confined
To the mean channels of no selfish mart,
Goes out to every shore
Of this broad earth, and throngs the sea with ships
That bear no thunders ; hushes hungry lips
In alien lands ;
Joins with a delicate web remotest strands ;
And gladdening rich and poor,
Doth gild Parisian domes,
Or feed the cottage smoke of English homes,
And only bounds its blessings by mankind !
In offices like these, thy mission lies,
My country ! and it shall not end
As long as rain shall fall and Heaven bend
In blue above thee ; though thy foes be hard
And cruel as their weapons, it shall guard
Thy hearth-stones as a bulwark ; make thee great
In white and bloodless state ;
And haply, as the years increase—
Still working through its humbler reach
With that large wisdom which the ages teach—
Revive the half dead dream of universal peace !

As men who labor in that mine
Of Cornwall, hollowed out beneath the bed
Of ocean, when a storm rolls overhead,

Hear the dull booming of the world of brine
Above them, and a mighty muffled roar
Of winds and waters, yet toil calmly on,
And split the rocks, and pile the massive ore,
Or carve a niche, or shape the archèd roof ;
So I, as calm, weave my woof
Of song, chanting the days to come,
Unsilenced, though the quiet summer air
Stirs with the bruit of battles, and each dawn
Wakes from its starry silence to the hour
Of many gathering armies. Still,
In that we sometimes hear,
Upon the northern winds, the voice of woe
Not wholly drowned in triumph, though I know
The end must crown us, and a few brief years
Dry all our tears,
I may not sing too gladly. To thy will,
Resigned, O Lord ! we all forget
That there is much even victory must regret.
And, therefore, not too long
From the great burthen of our country's wrong
Delay our just release !
And if it may be, save
These sacred fields of peace
From stain of patriot or of hostile blood !
Oh, help us, Lord ! to roll the crimson flood
Back on its course, and, while our banners wing
Northward, strike with us ! till the Goth shall cling
To his own blasted altar-stones ; and crave
Mercy ; and we shall grant it, and dictate
The lenient future of his fate
There, where some rotting ships and crumbling quays
Shall one day mark the Port which ruled the Western seas.

PAUL HAMILTON HAYNE.

Acquaintance with the winning personality of Hayne is not one of the least enjoyments to be gained from the study of American poetry. Paul Hamilton Hayne was born at Charleston, S. C., January 1, 1830. He was graduated at the University of South Carolina, started to practise law, and then became an editor. He has published several volumes of poems; but, like Lanier and Timrod, he found a poet's life necessitous. Hayne has written war lyrics, but he excelled in domestic sketches and in short pieces of quiet reflection on the subject of natural landscape, having the feeling of contentment that must precede repose in poetry. The two poems following are examples of the two styles. Hayne died at Copse Hill, Forest Station, Ga., July 6, 1886.

SONNET.

Here friend! upon this lofty ledge sit down!
And view the beauteous prospect spread below,
Around, above us; in the noon-day glow
How calm the landscape rests!—yon distant town,

Enwreathed with clouds of foliage like a crown
Of rustic honor; the soft, silvery flow
Of the clear stream beyond it, and the show
Of endless wooded heights, arching the brown
Autumnal fields, alive with billowy grain;
Say! hast thou ever gazed on aught more fair
In Europe, or the Orient ?—what domain
(From India to the sunny slopes of Spain)
Hath beauty wed to grandeur in the air,
Blessed with an ampler charm, a more benignant reign?

A LITTLE SAINT.

At the calm matin hour
  I see her bend in prayer,
As bends a virgin flower
  Kissed by the summer air.
O! meek the downcast eyes!
  But the sweet lips wear a smile;
How hard the little angel tries
  To be serious all the while!

I tell her 't is not right
  To be half grave, half gay,
Imploring in Heaven's sight
  A blessing on the day:
She hears and looks devout
  (Although it gives her pain);
Still, when the ritual 's almost out,
  She 's sure to smile again!

She shocks her maiden aunt,
  Who thinks it a disgrace
That—do her best—she can't
  Give her a solemn face:

She 'll scold, and rate, and fume,
  And lecture hour by hour,
Until she makes the very room
  Look passionate and sour!

Alack! 't is all in vain!
  Soon as the sermon's done,
My fairy blooms again,
  Like a rosebud in the sun;
I can not damp her mirth,
  I will not check her play,—
Is innocent joy so rife on earth
  Hers should not have full sway?

I asked her yester-night,
  Why, when prayer was made,
Her brow of cordial light
  Scarce caught one serious shade.
"Father," she said, "*you* love
  Better to meet me glad,
And so I thought the Christ above
  Might grieve to see me sad!"

HELEN HUNT JACKSON.

Helen Hunt Jackson was born at Amherst, Mass., October 18, 1831. Mrs. Jackson was the author of graceful stories and clever travel sketches, but she also wrote verse. Some of her poetry is warm and glowing in its associations, as in *The Riviera*; some of it is philosophical in aim, as in *Doubt*. Mrs. Jackson died at San Francisco, August 12, 1885.

THE RIVIERA.[1]

O peerless shore of peerless sea,
Ere mortal eye had gazed on thee,
What god was lover first of thine,
Drank deep of thy unvintaged wine,
And lying on thy shining breast
Knew all thy passion and thy rest ;
And when thy love he must resign,
O generous god, first love of thine,
Left such a dower of wealth to thee,
Thou peerless shore of peerless sea !
Thy balmy air, thy stintless sun,

[1] *The Riviera*, a name given to two portions of the coast of the Mediterranean on either side of Genoa.

Thy orange-flowering never done,
Thy myrtle, olive, palm, and pine,
Thy golden figs, thy ruddy wine,
Thy subtle and resistless spell
Which all men feel and none can tell !
Oh peerless shore of peerless sea !
From all the world we turn to thee ;
No wonder deem we thee divine
Some god was lover first of thine.

DOUBT.

They bade me cast the thing away,
They pointed to my hands all bleeding,
They listened not to all my pleading ;
　　The thing I meant I could not say ;
　　I knew that I should rue the day
　　If once I cast that thing away.

I grasped it firm, and bore the pain ;
The thorny husks I stripped and scattered ;
If I could reach its heart, what mattered
　　If other men saw not my gain,
　　Or even if I should be slain ?
　　I knew the risks ; I chose the pain.

Oh had I cast that thing away,
I had not found what most I cherish,
A faith without which I should perish,—
　　The faith which, like a kernel, lay
　　Hid in the husks which on that day
　　My instinct would not throw away !

BRET HARTE.

Bret Harte was born at Albany, N. Y., August, 1839. He early began the work of a man of letters, and has been a voluminous author. His greater reputation and production as a writer of romance hide his gifts as a poet; but if his noted and noteworthy poems be counted up, they make no mean showing. Of these, *John Burns* and *How Are You, Sanitary!* deal with certain of the less gloomy aspects of life in the civil war. *Plain Language from Truthful James* is a sportive squib at the Chinese. *Her Letter* is characterized by California simplicity of manners and feeling. *Dickens in Camp* is the most touching of Harte's poems. *The Angelus*, however, is the most poetical, reviving the dreamy romance of California's past.

THE ANGELUS.

(*Heard at the Mission Dolores,*[1] 1868.)

Bells of the past, whose long forgotten music
 Still fills the wide expanse,
Tingeing the sober twilight of the present
 With color of romance!

---

[1] *Mission Dolores*, an old Spanish Mission in San Francisco.

I hear your call, and see the sun descending
　On rock and wave and sand,
As down the coast the Mission voices blending,
　Girdle the heathen land.

Within the circle of your incantation
　No blight nor mildew falls ;
Nor fierce unrest, nor lust, nor low ambition
　Passes those airy walls.

Borne on the swell of your long waves receding,
　I touch the farther Past,—
I see the dying glow of Spanish glory,
　The sunset dream and last !

Before me rise the dome-shaped Mission towers,
　The white Presidio ;
The swart commander in his leathern jerkin,
　The priest in stole of snow.

Once more I see Portala's ¹ cross uplifting
　Above the setting sun ;
And past the headland, northward, slowly drifting
　The freighted galleon.

O solemn bells ! whose consecrated masses
　Recall the faith of old,—
O tinkling bells ! that lulled with twilight music
　The spiritual fold.

Your voices break and falter in the darkness,—
　Break, falter, and are still ;
And veiled and mystic, like the Host decending,
　The sun sinks from the hill !

¹ *Portala's Cross.*　See Harte's poem on the subject, *Overland Monthly.* vol. 3.

EDWARD ROWLAND SILL.

Edward Rowland Sill was born at Windsor, Conn., April 29, 1841. He was graduated at Yale, and engaged in varied work, finally becoming professor of English literature at the University of California. He died at Cleveland, Ohio, February 27, 1887. Sill wrote long poems, but like many other poets he is at his best in his shorter productions. When he has risen into thoughtfulness out of a certain excessive consciousness, in his expression, of pain, difficulty, or other emotion that sometimes mars his technical execution, his verse has an edge and force that is incisive and significant.

THE FOOL'S PRAYER.

The Royal feast was done ; the King
   Sought out some new sport to banish care,
And to his jester cried : " Sir Fool,
   Kneel down and make for us a prayer ! "

The jester doffed his cap and bells,
   And stood the mocking court before ;

They could not see the bitter smile
Behind the painted grin he wore.

He bowed his head and bent his knee
Upon the monarch's silken stool ;
His pleading voice arose : " O Lord,
Be merciful to me, a fool !

" No pity, Lord, could change the heart
From red with wrong to white as wool ;
The rod must heal the sin ; but Lord,
Be merciful to me a fool !

" 'T is not by guilt the onward sweep
Of truth and right, O Lord, we stay ,
'T is by our follies that so long
We hold the earth from heaven away.

" These clumsy feet, still in the mire,
Go crushing blossoms without end ;
These hard well-meaning hands we thrust
Among the heart-strings of a friend.

" The ill-timed truth we might have kept—
Who knows how sharp it pierced and stung ?
The word we had not sense to say—
Who knows how grandly it had rung?

" Our faults no tenderness should ask,
The chastening stripes must cleanse them all ;
But for our blunders—oh, in shame
Before the eyes of heaven we fall.

" Earth bears no balsam for mistakes ;
  Men crown the knave and scourge the tool
That did his will; but Thou, O Lord,
  Be merciful to me, a fool ! "

The room was hushed ; in silence rose
  The King, and sought his gardens cool,
And walked apart, and murmured low,
  " Be merciful to me, a fool ! "

JOAQUIN MILLER.

No general account of American literature can be complete without some mention of Joaquin Miller. Cincinnatus Hiner Miller, was born in the Wabash District, Ind., November 10, 1841. From 1854 on he lived in Oregon or California, being an editor in Oregon and for four years County Judge there. Having visited Europe in 1870, he published *Songs of the Sierras*. Other volumes have followed, among them *The Danites*, which has a merit that seems now unusual for a literary play, that of being successful on the stage.

Almost from the very outset of Miller's career, it was evident that his genius was larger than his literary surroundings. His earlier Californian verse was the prelude to the wider, richer note of *Songs of the Sierras* and *Songs of the Sunlands*. Among Miller's poems it is not easy, both on account of his range and of his prolificness, to make a choice for the purpose of commentary. Among other productions may well be selected, however, his pictures of the flying journey by rail across the American continent, his tales of pioneer adventure, and his idyl, the scene of which is laid upon the Amazon. Miller's power

would not have been shown but for his longer
poems, although the more critical reader may pre-
fer the shorter ones. Of the latter, *In Yosemite
Valley* is onomatopoetic, keenly descriptive, and
strongly, though perhaps a little dimly, reverential.
Charity is an original treatment of a favorite subject
in painting and poetry and contains some fine single
lines. On the whole, Miller's poems show a genius
which even yet has probably not fully developed
itself.

AT BETHLEHEM.

" In the desert a fountain is springing,
  In the wild waste there still is a tree."

" Though the many lights dwindle to one light,
  There is help if the heavens have one."

" Change lays not her hand upon truth."

With incense and myrrh and sweet spices,
Frankincense and sacredest oil
In ivory, chased with devices
Cut quaint and in serpentine coil ;
Heads bared and held down to the bosom ;
Brows massive with wisdom and bronzed ;
Beards white as the white may in blossom,
And borne to the breast and beyond,—
Came the Wise of the East, bending lowly
On staffs, with garments girt round
With girdles of hair, to the Holy

Child Christ, in their sandals.   The sound
Of song and thanksgiving ascended—
Deep night !   Yet some shepherds afar
Heard a wail with the worshiping blended
And they then knew the sign of the star.

IN YOSEMITE VALLEY.

Sound ! sound ! sound !
O colossal walls as crown'd
In one eternal thunder !
Sound ! sound ! sound !
O ye oceans overhead,
While we walk, subdued in wonder,
In the ferns and grasses, under
And beside the swift Merced ! [1]

Fret ! fret ! fret !
Streaming, sounding banners, set
On the giant granite castles
In the clouds and in the snow !
But the foe he comes not yet,—
We are loyal, valiant vassals,
And we touch the trailing tassels
Of the banners far below.

Surge ! surge ! surge !
From the white Sierra's verge,
To the very valley blossom.
Surge ! surge ! surge !

[1] *Merced*, a river in California, rising in the Sierra Nevadas, and flowing into the San Joaquin.

Yet the song-bird builds a home,
And the mossy branches cross them,
And the tasselled tree-tops toss them,
In the clouds of falling foam.

Sweep ! sweep ! sweep !
O ye heaven-born and deep,
In one dread, unbroken chorus !
We may wonder or may weep,—
We may wait on God before us ;
We may shout or lift a hand,—
We may bow down or deplore us,
But may never understand.

Beat ! beat ! beat !
We advance, but would retreat
From this restless, broken breast
Of the earth in a convulsion.
We would rest, but dare not rest,
For the angel of expulsion
From this Paradise below
Waves us onward and—we go.

CHARITY.

Her hands were clasped downward and doubled.
  Her head was held down and depressed,
Her bosom, like white billows troubled,
  Fell fitful and rose in unrest.

Her robes were all dust and disorder'd
  Her glory of hair and her brow,
Her face, that had lifted and lorded,
  Fell pallid and passionless now.

She heard not accusers that brought her
  In mockery hurried to Him,
Nor heeded, nor said, nor besought her
  With eyes lifted doubtful and dim.

All crush'd and stone-cast in behavior,
  She stood as a marble would stand,
Then the Saviour bent down, and the Saviour
  In silence wrote on in the sand.

What wrote He ?   How fondly one lingers
  And questions, what holy command
Fell down from the beautiful fingers
  Of Jesus, like gems in the sand.

O better the Scian ¹ uncherished
  Had died ere a note or device
Of battle was fashioned, than perished
  This only line written by Christ.

He arose and he look'd on the daughter
  Of Eve, like a delicate flower,
And he heard the revilers that brought her—
  Men stormy and strong as a tower ;

And he said : "She has sinn'd ; let the blameless
  Come forward and cast the first stone ! "
But they, they fled shamed and yet shameless ;
  And she, she stood white and alone.

¹ *Scian*, Homer, the greatest Greek poet, born perhaps at Chios, on the island of Scio.

Who now shall accuse and arraign us?
 What man shall condemn and disown?
Since Christ has said only the stainless
 Shall cast at his fellows a stone.

For what man can bare us his bosom,
 And touch, with his forefinger there,
And say, 'T is as snow, as a blossom?
 Beware of the stainless, beware!

O woman, both first to believe us;
 Yea, also born first to forget;
Born first to betray and deceive us,
 Yet first to repent and regret!

O first then in all that is human,
 Lo! first where the Nazarene trod,
O woman! O beautiful woman!
 Be then first in the kingdom of God!

PALATINE HILL.

I.

A wolf-like stream without a sound
 Steals by and hides beneath the shore,
 Its awful secrets evermore
Within its sullen bosom bound.

II.

And this was Rome, that shrieked for room
 To stretch her limbs; a hill of caves
 For half wild beasts and hairy slaves;
And gypsies bent within the tomb.

III.

Two lone palms on the Palatine,
  Two rows of cypress black and tall
  With white roots set in Cæsar's hall,—
A garden, convent, and sweet shrine.

IV.

Tall cedars on a broken wall,
  That look away toward Lebanon ! [1]
  And seem to mourn for grandeur gone :
A wolf, an owl,—and that is all.

A NUBIAN FACE ON THE NILE.

One night we touched the lily shore,
And then passed on, in night indeed,
Against the far white waterfall.
I saw no more, shall know no more.
Of her for aye.   And you who read
This broken bit of dream will smile,
Half vexed that I saw aught at all.
The waves struck strophes on the shore
And all the sad song of the oar
That long, long night against the Nile,
Was : Nevermore and nevermore
This side that shadowy shore that lies
Below the leafy paradise.

[1] *Lebanon*, a mountain chain of Syria, having a grove of venerable cedars at its summit.

CHARLES WARREN STODDARD.

Charles Warren Stoddard was born at Rochester, N. Y., August 7, 1843. He has been an active newspaper correspondent and has taught at a university in Indiana. His contributions to poetry are interesting and characteristic. He published at San Francisco in 1867 his first volume of verses. Among its contents is the vivid and faithful description of Mount Tamalpais, which is the highest peak rising from San Francisco Bay.

TAMALPAIS.[1]

How manifold thy beauties are !
I do not reckon time or space—
I worship thy exceeding grace,
And hasten as a flying star
To reach thy splendor from afar.

The first flush of thy morning face
Is dear to me ; thy shadowless
Broad noon that doth all sweets confess ;

[1] *Tamalpais*, a mountain in Marin County, California, of surpassing loveliness.

But fairer is thy even fall,
Which seems to cry with airy call
Thy roses in the wilderness,
Thy deserts blithely blossoming,
Decoy me for the love of spring.
With all thy grace and glitter spent,
Thy quiet dusk so eloquent ;
Thy vail of vapors—the caress
Of Zephyrus right cool and sweet—
I cannot wait to love thee less—
I cling to thee with full content,
And fall a dreaming at thy feet.

Anon the sudden evening gun,
Awakes me to the sinking sun
And golden glories at the Gate. [1]
The full, strong tides, that slowly run
Their sliding waters modulate
To indolent soft winds that wait
And lift a long net newly spun.
I see the groves of scented bay,
And night is in their fragrant May.
But tassel shadows swing and sway,
Upon their glimmering leaves of grass—
And there a fence of rail, quite gray,
With ribs of sunlight in the glass—
And here a branch full well arrayed
With struggling beams a moment stay'd—
Like panting butterflies afraid.

Lo !   Shadows slipping down the slope
And filling every narrow vale,

[1] *The Gate*, The Golden Gate.

The shining waters growing pale—
The mellow-burning star of Hope,
And in the wave its silver trope.
A slender shallop, feather-frail,
A pencil mast and rocking sail.
The glooms that gather at the Gate ;
The sombre lines against the sky,
While dizzy gnats about me fly,
And overhead the birds go by,
Dropping a note so crystal clear,
The spirit cannot choose but hear.
The hollow moon, and up between
An oak with yard-long mosses, green
In sunlight now as dull as crape ;
The mountain softened in its shape,
Its perfect symmetry attained—
And swathed in velvet folds, and stained
With dusky purple of the grape.

JOHN VANCE CHENEY.

John Vance Cheney was born at Groveland, N. Y., December 29, 1848. He has been teacher, lawyer, musician, and librarian; and has lived in Massachusetts, in New York City, and in San Francisco. Mr. Cheney has done work as a critic, and as a poet. His volume of critical essays, *The Golden Guess*, taking high ground as to the matter of poetry, has been supplemented by later, separate papers on other poets than those treated in that volume. His books of poetry are named modestly *Thistle-Drift* and *Wood-Blooms*. Mr. Cheney has excelled as a poet on several sides. His *Old Farm Barn* shows his aptitude at a homely scene. He has given more attention, however, thus far to daintier art, as in *The Way of It*. He has also treated sombre subjects, usually in poems with an undercurrent of suggestion beneath the description, such as *On the Ways of the Night*

THE WAY OF IT.

The wind is awake, little leaves, little leaves,
Heed not what he says—he deceives, he deceives :
Over and over

To the lowly clover
He has lisped the same love (and forgotten it, too)
He will soon be lisping and pledging to you.

The boy is abroad, dainty maid, dainty maid,
Beware his soft words—I 'm afraid, I 'm afraid ;
    He has said them before
    Times many a score,
Ay, he died for a dozen, ere his beard pricked through,
And the very same death he will die for you.

The way of the boy is the way of the wind,
As light as the leaves is dainty maid-kind ;
    One to deceive
    And one to believe—
That is the way of it, year to year,
But I know you will learn it too late, my dear.

ON THE WAYS OF THE NIGHT.

Who did it, Fall wind, sighing,
    Who struck her cheek so white ?
Why gathers she the wild waves flying
    On the ways of night ?

No longer let her wander,
    Poor ghost, that she should freeze !
Tell her, help her over yonder
    To the tender trees.

Th' unpitying, bitter weather !
    Ere moon and stars be dead,
Blow the yellow leaves together,
    Make the maid a bed.

JAMES HERBERT MORSE.

James Herbert Morse was born at Hubbardston, Mass., October 8, 1841. He was graduated at Harvard, and became a successful teacher in New York. His first volume, entitled *Summer-Haven Songs*, was published in 1886. He has been a regular contributor to the *Atlantic*, the *Critic*, and other literary journals. Among his single poems, *Loss*, though short, is a good example of the author's poetic quality. *Mazzini* is an appreciative character picture. Morse's verse is often characterized by the utmost poetical delicacy and susceptibility, and he has the rare gift of saying much in few words.

MAZZINI.

His soul wrought long and wore the flesh away,
But kept a shining edge, like brightest steel,
That by its fearless strokes made nations feel
What inward rottenness and swift decay

Under the foot of social error lay ;—
Ay, made them feel the centre-piercing pain

That lies about the birth of every gain,
And makes the day of joy a wrathful day.

Now, worn, quite worn, the scabbard old,
The eye that lent its fire, the nerves so tense,
The ready hand so firm—there darkly mould,
And waste into their primal elements.

And we, who saw where these brave things were laid,
Ask vainly for that finely-polished blade.

JOHN BOYLE O'REILLY.

The name of John Boyle O'Reilly is recognized
in American literature as synonymous with the word
heart. O'Reilly was born at Dowth Castle, Meath,
Ireland, January 28, 1844. Committed, unfortu-
nately, to imprisonment in Australia, on a political
charge, he escaped and came to this country, making
his home in Boston, where he has published several
volumes of poems. He died at Hull, Mass., August
10, 1890.

O'Reilly has many gifts in the matter of poetry—
keen analysis, an eye for landscape, and sharp, vivid
expression ; but, more than anything else, stands out
his sure, sententious judgment of character.

THREE GRAVES.

How did he live, this dead man here,
With the temple above his grave ?
He lived as a great one, from cradle to bier
He was nursed in luxury, trained in pride,—
When the wish was born, it was gratified ;
Without thanks he took, without heed he gave.

The common man was to him a clod,
From whom he was far as a demigod.
His duties ? To see that his rents were paid.
His pleasures ? To know that the crowd obeyed.
His pulse, if you felt it, throbbed apart,
With a separate stroke from the people's heart.
But whom did he love, and whom did he bless ?
Was the life of him more than a man's, or less ?
I know not. He died, there was none to blame,
And as few to weep ; but these marbles came
For the temple that rose to preserve his name !

How did he live, that other dead man,
From the graves apart and alone ?
As a great one too ? Yes, this was one
Who lived to labor and study and plan.
The earth's deep thought he loved to reveal ;
He banded the breast of the land with steel ;
The thread of his foil he never broke ;
He filled the cities with wheels and smoke,
And workers by day, and workers by night,
For the day was too short for his vigor's flight,
Too firm was he to be feeling and giving ;
For labor, for gain, was a life worth living.
He worshipped industry, dreamt of her, sighed for her ;
Potent he grew by her, famous he died for her.
They say he improved the world in his time,
That his mills and mines were a work sublime.
When he died—the laborers rested and sighed ;
Which was it—because he had lived or died ?

And how did he live, that dead man there,
In the country churchyard laid ?
Oh, he? He came for the sweet field air ;

He was tired of the town, and he took no pride
In its fashion or fame.   He returned and died
In the place he loved, where a child he played
With those who have knelt by his grave and prayed.
He ruled no serfs, and he knew no pride,
He was with the workers side by side ;
He hated a mill, and a mine, and a town,
With their fever of misery, struggle, renown ;
He could never believe but a man was made
For a nobler end than the glory of trade ;
For the youth he mourned with an endless pity
Who were cast like snow on the streets of the city.

He was weak, maybe ; but he lost no friend ;
Who loved him once, loved on to the end.
He mourned all selfish and vain endeavor ;
But he never injured a weak one—never.
When censure was passed, he was kindly dumb ;
He was never so wise but a fault would come ;
He was never so old that he failed to enjoy
The games and the dreams he had loved when a boy ;
He erred and was sorry ; but never drew
A trusting heart from the pure and true.
When friends look back from the years to be,
God grant they may say such things of me.

RICHARD WATSON GILDER.

Richard Watson Gilder, editor of the *Century Magazine*, was born at Bordentown, N. J., February 8, 1844. At the age of nineteen he did artillery service in the war. Afterwards he became a journalist, then editor of the *Century Magazine*. Mr. Gilder has published several volumes of verse, giving evidence of a bold, vigorous personality, and of a fine nature, receptive to the higher influences. *"Oh! Love is Not a Summer Mood,"* is a poem where his conceptions are at their purest.

"OH! LOVE IS NOT A SUMMER MOOD."

I.

Oh, Love is not a summer mood,
Nor flying phantom of the brain,
Nor youthful fever of the blood,
Nor dream, nor fate, nor circumstance.
Love is not born of blinded chance,
Nor bred in simple ignorance.

II.

But love hath winter in her blood,
And love is fruit of holy pain,
And perfect flower of maidenhood.
True love is steadfast as the skies,
And once alight she never flies ;
And love is strong, and still, and wise.

GEORGE PARSONS LATHROP.

George Parsons Lathrop was born at Oahu, Hawaiian Islands, August 25, 1851. He studied in New York and at Dresden from 1867 to 1870. He has devoted himself to literature, and has published several volumes of poems. The selection below is an ode of broad, patriotic spirit, one of his best productions in verse.

STRIKE HANDS, YOUNG MEN!

Strike hands, young men !
We know not when
Death or disaster comes,
Mightier than battle-drums
To summon us away.
Death bids us say farewell
To all we love, nor stay
For tears ;—and who can tell
How soon misfortune's hand
May smite us where we stand,
Dragging us down, aloof,
Under the swift world's hoof ?

Strike hands for faith, and power
To gladden the passing hour ;
To wield the sword, or raise a song ;
To press the grape ; or crush out wrong,
And strengthen right.
Give me the man of sturdy palm
And vigorous brain ;
Hearty, companionable, sane,
'Mid all commotions calm,
Yet filled with quick, enthusiastic fire ;
Give me the man
Whose impulses aspire,
And all his features seem to say, " I can ! "

Strike hands, young men !
'T is yours to help rebuild the state,
And keep the nation great.
With act, and speech, and pen
'T is yours to spread
The morning-red
That ushers in a grander day ;
To scatter prejudice that blinds,
And hail fresh thoughts in noble minds ;
To overthrow bland tyrannies
That cheat the people, and with slow disease
Change the Republic to a mockery,
Your words can teach that liberty
Means more than just to cry " We 're free,"
While bending to some new-found yoke.
So shall each unjust band be broke,
Each toiler gain his meet reward
And life sound forth a truer chord.

Ah, if we so have striven
And mutually the grasp have given
Of brotherhood,
To work each other and the whole race good :
What matter if the dream
Come only partly true,
And all the things accomplished seem
Feeble and few ?
At least, when summer's flame burns low
And on our heads the drifting snow
Settles and stays,
We shall rejoice that in our earlier days
We boldly then
Struck hands, young men !

JAMES WHITCOMB RILEY.

James Whitcomb Riley was born at Granfield, Ind., in 1853. He first essayed the trade of a sign painter, then joined a company of strolling players. Afterwards he became a journalist and a lecturer.

Riley is most generally known by his verse in dialect, which forms the greater part of his volumes of poems. He has reached, however, no mean attainment in more literary and purer English, which, if he can use with as good effect, may be granted to be of itself a better vehicle. *The Orchard Lands of Long Ago* and *Our Kind of a Man* give evidence that Riley's powers are equal to the production of something beyond merely local and ephemeral verse.

THE ORCHARD LANDS OF LONG AGO.

The orchard lands of Long Ago!
O drowsy winds, awake, and blow
The snowy blossoms back to me,
And all the buds that used to be!
Blow back along the grassy ways
Of truant feet, and lift the haze
Of happy summer from the trees
That trail their tresses in the seas

Of grain that float and overflow
The orchard lands of Long Ago !

Blow back the melody that slips
In lazy laughter from the lips
That marvel much if any kiss,
Is sweeter than the apples' is.
Blow back the twitter of the birds—
The lisp, the titter, and the words
Of merriment that found the shine
Of summer-time a glorious wine
That drenched the leaves that loved it so,
In orchard lands of Long Ago !

O memory ! alight and sing
Where rosy bellied pippins cling,
And golden russets glint and gleam,
As in the old Arabian dream,
The fruits of that enchanted tree
The glad Aladdin robbed for me.
And, drowsy winds, awake and fan
My blood as when it overran
A heart ripe as the apples grow
In orchard lands of Long Ago !

OUR KIND OF A MAN.

I.

The kind of a man for you and me !
He faces the world unflinchingly
And smites as long as the wrong resists,
With a knuckled faith and force like fists !
He lives the life he is preaching of,

And loves where most is the need of love ;
His voice is clear to the deaf man's ears
And his face sublime through the blind man's tears.
The light shines out where the clouds were dim,
And the widow's prayer goes up for him ;
The latch is clicked at the hovel door,
And the sick man sees the sun once more,
And out o'er the barren fields he sees
Springing blossoms and waving trees,
Feeling, as only the dying may,
That God's own servant has come that way,
Smoothing the path as it still winds on
Through the golden gate where the loved have gone.

II.

The kind of a man for you and me !
However little of work we do
He credits full, and abides in trust
That time will teach us how more is just.
He walks abroad, and he meets all kinds
Of querulous and uneasy minds,
And, sympathizing, he shares the pain
Of the doubts that rack us, heart and brain ;
And, knowing this, as we grasp his hand,
We are surely coming to understand !
He looks on sin with pitying eyes—
E'en as the Lord, since Paradise,—
Else, should we read, 'Though our sins should glow
As scarlet, they shall be white as snow ?—
And feeling still with a grief half glad,
That the bad are as good as the good are bad,
He strikes out straight for the Right—and he
Is the kind of a man for you and me !

EDITH MATILDA THOMAS.

Edith Matilda Thomas was born at Chatham, Ohio, in 1854. She was educated at a normal school, and has written poems which have gained popularity. Miss Thomas's chief merit in verse is her style, which includes classical spirit, varied emotion, and fresh use of words. Her characteristic fault is that she does not usually subordinate clearly the numerous ideas of a poem to one dominant connection. In such a poem, however, as the *Sea-Bird and Land-Bird* her art attains harmony of purpose.

SEA-BIRD AND LAND-BIRD.

A land-bird would follow a sea-bird's flight,
Over the surges and out of sight,
It joyed to lave
In the bead of the wave,
And watched the great sky in its mirror glassed ;
And all was well
Till, with measureless swell,
Under the gale rose the waters vast,

Then, baffled and maimed,
With spirit tamed,
The bird 'mid the drift on the shore was cast.

Thou wast that sea-bird strong and light
(Shall a land-bird follow a sea-bird's flight ?)—
Wast fledged on high,
Close under the sky ;
The wandering cloud would sometimes bend
With billowy breast
Above thy nest,
And in pity moist her substance spend ;
No mate thou couldst find
Like the fierce North Wind,
And the tempest that tried thee most was thy friend !

I was that land-bird, frail and slight
(Shall a sea-bird stay for a land-bird's flight ?) ;
Low on the earth
I had my birth,
In a sunny field where the days were long ;
There as I lay
I heard the spray
Of the grass in June growing deep and strong ;
Fast the days flew,
And I followed, too ;
And saluted the sun with my slender song !

Hear me, thou sea-bird, matchless in flight,
Shaping thy course o'er the surges white !
In the making of things,
Strength fell to thy wings,
So that thou shouldst not falter nor tire

When beating abroad ;
The breath of a god
Was breathed through thy form,—and enduring fire.
To me, out of heaven,
No fire was given,
Nor strength, but only the rover's desire.

Shall a land-bird follow a sea-bird's flight,
Over the surges and out of sight?
The Maker of things
Has touched my wings
And taken from me my blind unrest !
Now am I blent
With the fields content,
In the grassy deep where I make my nest.—
Say can'st thou hear,
My carol clear,—
Thou, by the soundful sea oppressed ?

19

GEORGE EDWARD WOODBERRY.

George Edward Woodberry was born at Beverly, Mass., May 12, 1855. He was graduated at Harvard, and became professor first at the University of Nebraska, later at Columbia College; he has also been connected with the New York *Nation*. Mr. Woodberry has published a history of wood-engraving, and a life of Poe. *Studies in Life and Letters* is a volume characterized, among American essays of the day, not only by a true "interest in ideal living" as fed from contemporary sources, but by the presence of not a few elements, firmly grasped, of spiritual wisdom. Those in America who are idealists either in hope or fact may find these essays useful as a guide to the appreciation and better understanding of its author's volume of poetry entitled *The North Shore Watch, and Other Poems*. Woodberry is a poet of patriotism in such verse as *Our First Century*; while the poems *At Gibraltar* and *To Leo XIII.* show that he possesses, further, the steadfast moral quality of the English race, with its warlike Scandinavian feeling.

OUR FIRST CENTURY.

It cannot be that men who are the seed
Of Washington should miss fame's true applause ;
Franklin did plan us ; Marshall gave us laws ;
And slow the broad scroll grew a people's creed,—
One land and free ! then at our dangerous need
Time's challenge coming, Lincoln gave it pause,
Upheld the ample pillars of the cause,
And dying left them whole—the crowning deed.
Such was the fathering race that made all fast,
Who founded us, and spread from sea to sea
A thousand leagues the zone of liberty,
And built for man this refuge from his past,
Unkinged, unchurched, unsoldiered, shamed were we,
Failing the stature that such sires forecast.

TO LEO XIII.

The German tyrant plays thee for his game ;
Italy curbs thee ; France gives little rest ;
And o'er the broad sea dost thou think to tame
God's young plantation in the virgin West ?
Three kingdoms did He sift to find the seed,
And sowed ; then open threw the sea's wide door ;
And millions came, used but to starve and bleed,
And built the great republic of the poor.

Remember Dover Strait that shore from thee
Whole empires, hidden in the banked-up clouds
Of England's greatness ! Of all lands are we,
But chiefly Northmen ; still their might enshrouds
The fates ; dream not their children of this sod
Cease to be freemen when they bow to God.

HELEN GRAY CONE.

Helen Gray Cone was born at New York, March 8, 1859. She was graduated from the New York Normal College, and became teacher there. Miss Cone has published two volumes of verse. In some of her poems there are remarkable gleams of poetic insight, but her best attainment has been in fancy rather than in imagination. Among single poems, *The Spring Beauties* is especially distinctive in its blending of close observation and pleasant moralizing.

THE SPRING BEAUTIES.

The Puritan Spring Beauties stood freshly clad for church ;
A thrush, white-breasted, o'er them sat singing on his perch.
"Happy be! for fair are ye!" the gentle singer told them,
But presently a buff-coat Bee came booming up to scold them.

" Vanity, oh vanity !
Young maids beware of vanity ! "
Grumbled out the buff-coat Bee,
Half parson-like, half soldierly.

The sweet-faced maidens trembled, with pretty, pinky
    blushes,
Convinced that it was wicked to listen to the thrushes ;
And when, that shady afternoon, I chanced that way to
    pass,
They hung their little bonnets down and looked into the
    grass.
    All because the buff-coat Bee
    Lectured them so solemnly :—
      " Vanity, oh, vanity !
    Young maids, beware of vanity ! "

AN INVOCATION IN A LIBRARY.

O brotherhood, with bay-crowned brows undaunted,
    Who passed serene along our crowded ways,
Speak with us still ! For we, like Saul, are haunted :
    Harp sullen spirits from these later days !

Whate'er high hope ye had for man, your brother,
    Breathe it, nor leave him like a prisoned slave
To stare through bars upon a sight no other
    Than clouded skies that lighten on a grave.

In these still alcoves give us gentle meeting,
    From dusky shelves kind arms about us fold,
Till the New Age shall feel her chilled heart beating
    Restfully on the warm heart of the Old.

Till we shall hear your voices mild and winning
    Steal through our doubt and discord as outswells
At fiercest noon, above a city's dinning,
    The chiming music of cathedral bells !

Music that lifts the thought from trodden places
    And coarse confusions that around us lie,
Up to the calm of high cloud-silvered spaces
    Where the tall spire points through the soundless sky.

CLINTON SCOLLARD.

Clinton Scollard was born at Clinton, N. Y., September 18, 1860. He was graduated at Hamilton College, and became professor there. Mr. Scollard has published several volumes of verse. He has taken advantage of foreign travel to use uncommon as well as familiar themes. His poetry is graceful, and in *The Hunter* and *The Angler*, has also the fresh atmosphere and spirit of out-door nature.

THE HUNTER.

Through dewy glades ere morn is high,
When fleecy cloud-ships sail the sky,
   With buoyant step and gun a-shoulder,
And song on lip he wanders by.

He feels the cool air fan his brow,
He scents the spice of pine-tree bough,
   And lists from moss-encrusted boulder,
The thrush repeat her matin vow.

Afar he hears the ringing horn,
And, from the rustling fields of corn,
   The harvest music welling over,
Greeting the autumn day, new-born.

In pendant purple globes he sees
The wild grapes hang amid the trees,
   And, from the last red buds of clover,
The darting flight of golden bees.

He marks the fiery crimson gleam
On wide primeval woods that seem
   Like armored hosts with banners flying,
That march where weary warriors dream.

Before him long-eared rabbits pass
Like shadows, through the aisles of grass ;
   From copses, wren to wren replying,
Utter for him a morning mass.

He does not heed the partridge's drum,
The squirrel's chattering, nor the hum
   Of myriad noises that, incessant,
Down dusky forest arches come.

He crosses quiet nooks of shade,
With flickering sunshine interlaid,
   Where, when outshines the silvery crescent,
Flit by the pixies, half afraid.

Thus on and on he blithely speeds,
Through briery brake and tangled reeds,
   Thinking of Robin [1] and his bowmen,
And all the archer's daring deeds ;

Till 'neath a slope by vines o'ergrown,
Where, in the ages that have flown,
   The redmen slew their swarthy foemen,
He stands beside a pool, alone.

[1] *Robin Hood*, a famous English outlaw and huntsman, supposed to
have lived in the reign of Richard I.

Deep in a thicket, dense and dim,
That skirts the rushy water's rim,
  He crouches low and keenly listens
For sound of hoof or stir of limb.

At length he sees within the sheen
Of trembling leafage, darkly green,
  A lustrous eye that softly glistens,
And then a head of royal mien.

The startled hillsides sharply ring,
And answering echoes backward fling,
  While prone upon the earth before him,
A proud red deer lies quivering.

He swings his prize to shoulders strong,
Then homeward swiftly strides along,
  The great blue skies a-smiling o'er him,
And all around the birds in song.

Behind the woods the sun creeps down
And leaves thereon a crimson crown ;
  From sapphire portals, pale and tender,
Venus o'erlooks the meadows brown.

And now that shadows hide the lane
Where rolled the orchard-laden wain,
  His weary feet upon the fender,
He slays the red deer o'er again !

THE ANGLER.

He rises ere the dews at dawn
Like diamonds gleam upon the lawn ;
And down the fragrant pasture goes
Through buttercups and wild primrose ;

The bobolinks amid the grass
Laugh merrily to see him pass,
O foolish gossips in the mist,
He speeds to keep no morning tryst !

With fixed intent, he does not heed
The mottled moth, a fairy steed,
That seeks the wood till night enfold
The day, and steal its wealth of gold.
He gains the grove where woodbines twine
Around the boles of elm and pine
Nor pauses till he stands amid
The reeds where Pan the piper hid.

What joy is his to see the gleam
Of silvery fin within the stream,
To hold in leash each eager sense
With silence breathless and intense,
To mark an arrowy flash, and feel
The sudden pulsing of the reel,
As with electric current fine
He sends his nerve along the line.

Companioned by a keen desire
His sturdy patience does not tire ;
Through morning hours in sun or rain,
He smiles content with meagre gain ;
Breathing the perfect calm that broods,
In nature's secret solitudes,
Gleaning from river, wood, and sky,
A deep and broad philosophy.

MINNIE GILMORE.

Minnie Gilmore was born at Boston, Mass., 18—. She is the daughter of P. S. Gilmore, the well known musician. The graceful poem below, which was written at New York, is taken from Miss Gilmore's volume of poems, *Pipes from the Prairies*. Miss Gilmore is better known as a novelist than as a poet, by her stories, *A Son of Esau* and *The Woman That Stood Between*. The latter is a tale of the life of an anarchist. The former deals with society in a western State. Miss Gilmore is one of the few who have succeeded in the novel in bringing out the difference between Eastern and Western ethics and manners. In verse, her style has charm ; in the novel, charm and power.

THE DESERTED CHAPEL.

A chapel by the wayside
Silent and dark and chill ;
Out of the gloom, and the solemn hush,
The plaintive notes of a lonely thrush,
And wail of whippoorwill.

White on the untrod threshold,
    Daisies in virgin file ;
While stately grasses troop up in green,
And scaling the steps that intervene,
    Fade in the dusky aisle.

Silent within the belfry,
    A bell with shattered tongue ;
And swallows twit on the chancel eaves
Where wild vines clamber and twine their leaves
    The warm brown nests among.

O chapel by the wayside,
    And tales thy ruins tell !
Out of thy shadows pale phantoms dart—
Out of thy silence strange echoes start,
    O mute old iron bell !

Again the weary pilgrims
    Thine aisles tread as of yore ;
Again the toll, and the measured tread
Of patriot mourners who bear their dead
    Within thy shadowed door.

Again the pealing organ,
    The roses down thy nave ;
The laughing bells and the happy bride,
Who saw not lying the year beside
    This tiny, moss-grown grave.

DORA GOODALE.

Dora Read Goodale was born at Mount Washington, Mass., October 29, 1866. She and her elder sister, Elaine, wrote poetry young, and in 1878 published their first volume, *Apple Blossoms*, which was soon followed by other collections, entitled *In Berkshire with the Wild Flowers*, and *Verses from Sky Farm*. The poems are like their titles: fresh, naive, full of innocent happiness, and close observation of the surrounding nature. As was remarked by the reviewers, the poems of Dora and her sister were the productions of children who held the poet's pen.

A-BERRYING.

Down in the meadow's border-tangle,
  Heavy and still in the parching heat,
A little above the rugged angle
  Where the shadowy woods converge and meet,
Is a wall, with blackberry vines o'errun,
  Scarlet leaves, as the woodbine is,
Buttercups, all ablaze in the sun,
  Gypsy-daisies and clematis !

301

Here, as the restless winds pass over,
  The cat-bird swings in her thorny nest,
As the berry-girls by chance discover
  A callow stranger beside the rest !
Swallows, a-tilt on the lichened rail,
  Wait a little until you pass,
And the snake slips by and leaves a trail,
  Like to the wind in the meadow grass.

Into the sweet September weather,
  Under the searching harvest fires,
Lads and lassies go out together
  Eager to strip the bending briers ;
Boys of the mountains, one by one,
  Girls of the uplands, wild and sweet,
Gypsy-brown in the ardent sun,
  Scarlet-cheeked in the Autumn heat.

Breaking in through the thorny hedges,
  Singing and whistling, blithe and gay,
Wandering down to the woodland edges,
  Plucking asters along the way ;
Following back thro' the pasture bars,
  With the heavy baskets, two by two,
Under the lovely, distant stars,
  Into the darkness, into the dew.

THE END.

INDEX OF FIRST LINES.

INDEX.